THE TENTH GIRL

CARRIE AARONS

Editing done by Proofing Style.

Cover designed by Okay Creations.

Do you want your **FREE** Carrie Aarons eBook?

All you have to do is **sign up for my newsletter**, and you'll immediately receive your free book!

To Napoleon. Thanks for being the most loyal writing buddy an author could ask for.

PROLOGUE

CAIN

The competition was simple.

Four years.

Ten girls.

Winner got bragging rights and the key to The Atrium for the entire summer before we all went off to college.

It sounded easy when we drew up the terms, sealing the deal with a cheers around a table stacked with Bud Lights that Joshua had stolen from his older brother's stash. All six of the freshman who were recruited to the varsity football team had pledged their participation.

Fuck ten girls, preferably virgins but we weren't going to be picky, by the last day of our senior year of high school. The first one to ten won it all.

It sounded easy. Plus, we'd be getting off and what was better than that?

I'd done well for myself, scoring chicks and blow jobs alike. Even if I didn't do a dance in their end zone, getting my dick sucked wasn't a bad consolation prize.

Nine girls. I'd racked up a tally of nine, which in a high school of two thousand kids, was pretty hard to do if you thought about it. Girls talked to their friends, warned them off from assholes just trying to get in their pants. A lot of these girls didn't want to sleep with that many people, thought they'd be called a slut if their number got too high, too quickly.

But I'd managed to do it. It really hadn't been hard. Being the best high school quarterback in the state of Texas with charm that could melt rubber off tires helped a lot. Chicks were dying to brag about the one night they'd spent with me.

All I had to do was scratch number ten into my bedpost and that would be that. Victory would be mine.

From the moment I saw her, I knew she would be my final mark.

If only Harper Posy had been that simple. If only Harper Posy had been that easy.

1

HARPER

A dusty ranch home was a step up from the trailer park, but just barely.

The plumes of dirt clouds rose up behind the car as it pulled onto my grandmother's land, rolling green hills with clumps of forest creating a scene from a western movie right in front of my eyes.

For a Florida Keys girl, the lack of salty sea air was suffocating, the amount of greenery and the smell of horse manure souring my nose.

From the driver's seat, Mom steers as she chews her nail beds down to quick. I'm surprised they aren't bleeding yet, her most anxious moments always coming with the destruction of her manicure.

I'd hardly been able to pack my threadbare belongings from our trailer before she whisked us out on a sob and a heartbreak, her latest relationship going south and ousting us from the only home I'd ever known.

Sure, it had been a crappy home in a strung-out county of the hottest, muggiest location in the United States, but still ... it had been home.

"Harper Pearl Posy, did you even hear me?" Mom's southern twang lilts into my ears.

Is it me or does it sound stronger since we passed the border into her hometown, Haven, Texas?

"What's that?" I don't mask the attitude from my voice.

I don't mean to be a brat, my mom usually doesn't ask anything from me and as far as mothers go, she's a pretty great one. But ... I'm unusually bitter. I don't want to move to Texas, where football and cows are always on the menu. I liked my little corner of Florida, kayaking solo through the mangroves and writing in my journal on remote beaches.

"Don't slouch in front of your grandmother. And button that top button. She's going to make a comment about your ripped up jeans, but don't let her smell the fear on you."

I'm not sure why she's decided to come home after all of this time. Maybe it's because we're broke, although she never said anything. While my mom has a steady, good job, raising a child alone on an elementary school teacher's salary is almost impossible. We always had enough, but there were never any leftovers.

Could that be why we were going to live with my grandmother?

My grandmother was that in name only. Having met her only two times in my life, we weren't close. The first time was at my grandfather's funeral when I was seven, and I barely remember it. The other was when she came to Florida for Christmas five years ago and left early because she and my mom could barely stand to be in the same room. I could tell it was because her mother didn't approve of her choices, or getting pregnant with me once upon a time out of wedlock. I could also tell that it had been this way for probably their entire lives together.

We pull up to the front of the house, the yellow siding of the ranch caked in dust, just like our car. I wasn't sure how or why my grandmother still has all of this land, as the animals and production of hay and whatever else happens on a farm ceased when my grandfather died. I remember this detail, because I remember Mom and Grandma fighting over this on the phone for years.

But there she was, the strong-jawed woman, standing on the faded wood of the front steps, a German shepherd and a large sheep dog flanking her.

Mom pulls in to the sounds of a rooster cock-a-doodle-doing, and damn it's so Texas I almost have to roll my eyes. She takes a deep breath, squeezes my hand, and grips the door lock.

Once we get out of this car, our lives will have officially changed. No more Florida girls, getting through it just the two of us. We'll be in Texas. In the unknown, but so known for her. I'm scared, but the storyteller in me is excited to observe the new wide-open spaces around me. With each new corner of the world I find, I get a little more inspired to write.

We exit the car, the dry heat hitting me in the face with such force that I need to cough up a dusty lung.

"Hi, Mama," my own mother calls to her parent, her southern twang really making its grand entrance.

My grandmother nods, not moving any other muscle, and I swear, she could intimidate a mob boss, this woman.

But for some reason, she doesn't scare me. "Hi, Grandma. Thanks for having us."

Her lip curls up a little at my polite greeting, and I look into her eyes. Maybe it's because we're more alike than my mother and I are. In my grandmother, even if I haven't seen her in a long time, I find a kindred spirit. Where my mother is bubbly and lively, I am quiet and introverted. Where she is still wide-eyed at times, I'm realistic and can be blunt. I have a feeling that I have my grandmother to thank for those qualities.

We walk together to stand in front of her, and the sheep dog begins to lick my hand.

"You're too skinny, but some Texas meat will fix that right up. But, I see you received your mother's breasts. That will be a problem for a girl like you. A big bosom and long legs tempt men even if we don't want it too. You'll come to church with me every Sunday to remedy that."

She says this all matter-of-factly, as if I would just nod my head and agree. I cross my arms over my boobs, knowing full well that the C cups look odd on my small frame. And now I was more self-conscious about it than ever.

"Wow, Mama, can we at least move our bags from the trunk to the house first without talks of Holy Sunday?" Mom giggles, and I love her.

She could kill a dragon with kindness.

And with that, my grandmother is done with us, turning and walking into the house without offering a drink or showing us to our rooms. Mom pulls open the screen door as we drag our bags in, and I'm met with a home that hasn't left the nineteen seventies. Shag carpet, wood paneling on the walls, a TV that was discontinued thirty years ago, and that collection of Christmas plates resting on railings nailed into the drywall.

But it's clean, and bigger than the mobile home I grew up in, so I can't complain. Plus, I get my own room, and don't have to sleep on the convertible couch/table when Mom brings dates home, who almost sit on me while they kiss her. Maybe Texas ain't so bad.

I set my things out slowly from the one suitcase I brought with me. Two pairs of jeans, a couple of shirts, one pair of jean shorts and one white khaki, three dresses ranging in fanciness, a handful of underwear and bras, my favorite Agatha Christie novel with a worn and tattered cover, the only picture of my father I've ever seen, and my laptop. My entire life, there, laid out on the green plaid wool blanket on the twin bed I was to sleep in.

I run a finger down my father's cheek, the same high bone structure that he gave to me smiling back from under his firefighting hard hat. How is it possible to miss someone you hardly even remember?

My laptop is on its last leg, the keys worn off even though I know them by heart. I splurged all of the money I had on an external hard-drive last year, because God knows this thing is going to crash at some point and take my entire debut novel with it. I've been pouring my heart and soul into this book for the last three years, in between school and work, and I'm so close to finishing it, I can taste it.

By the time I walk out of my room, my stomach rumbling, it's dark and silent. And I mean *silent*. I make my way to the kitchen, to the huge sliding glass doors, and look out.

Pitch black.

Not a sound.

Weird ... I wasn't used to this. It wasn't bad, it was just different.

I had a feeling everything was about to be different. It started low in the stomach, like only those types of feeling can. Foreboding ran up and over my shoulders, prickling up my neck, alerting every hair follicle. Change was coming, even bigger than the one that was already here.

"Are you ready for school tomorrow?" A quiet, low voice speaks from my left.

I startle to find my grandmother sitting at the kitchen table, a mug cupped between her hands. Jesus, when did she get here? She was like a ninja, I hadn't even sensed her presence.

I nod, although I'm not. Of course Mom had driven us up here on a Sunday in the middle of September. Of course I would have to go to a brand new school as a senior just hours after I put down roots in Texas.

"I guess. I'm pretty good in school." I offer up this fact as if I want some sort of medal or cookie from her.

A flicker of a smirk ghosts her lips, and she rises. When she passes me, she places a hand on my shoulder.

"Don't let those rowdy Haven kids get the best of you. Welcome to Texas, girlie."

And with that she walks off, leaving me even more unsure than I already was.

2

HARPER

The hard-edged voice of Jason Aldean beats like a drum in my ears, my worn out earbuds stuck into the canals to drown out the anxiety coursing through my blood.

At least I wouldn't have to change my taste in music. Florida and Texas both had that redneck country vibe in common, so I was A-Okay when it came to staying hip on the latest tracks.

Haven High School was way nicer than the percentage of this town I'd seen already, and I remember Mom mentioning something about a big football donor putting a lot of money into the facility a couple of years back. And by putting a lot of money into it, she must have meant that the person literally paid to have a new state-of-the-art school constructed. New red brick and gleaming glass make up the school, with picnic tables and garden areas scattered on a quad outside. Beyond that is what has got to be one of the biggest sports stadiums I've ever seen, not that I've seen many, and this is a high school we're talking about. The turf is bright green, and every section of the track and facilities surrounding it is manicured.

Which makes me wonder, what did the other part of town look like? I was from the Keys; the part that tourists didn't venture into and was more frequented by dealers and smugglers. I knew there was always a different side of somewhere, and that I typically didn't belong there.

The parking lot is paved to perfection, with bright white lines sectioning off the spots. I decided to walk to school on my first day. Hell, who was I kidding? We could barely afford one car, and it wasn't like my family's house was that far from school. I enjoyed the fresh air and the silent time to think, to create stories in my head that I would one day write for the masses to read.

And because I'm so wrapped up in Sam Hunt and checking out the place that will be educating me for the next year, I almost don't see the Jeep barreling toward me.

At the very last second, I jump out of the way, the truck the only one in the parking lot. This maniac person the only one in the parking lot ... well, besides me.

I pop an earbud out and inspect the vehicle, pausing my music as I slow my walking. The car is one of those old-school, soft-top Jeeps, everything removed, with mud on the tires and specks of it dotting the white body of the frame. I can see inside, the weather in late September still scorching hot in Haven.

Black leather seats, with a gym bag and books scattered along the floor in the backseat. Which I can see ... since there are no doors on the entire car. And when I look up to see its owner ... I'm stunned.

A giant unfurls his long body from the car, lean legs followed by a thick torso, strong neck and jaw that lead up to a jet-black hairline. This boy, who looks more like a man, is muscled from his head to his toes, you can tell by the way his jeans pull tight on that sculpted behind and his biceps strain in the plain green T-shirt. That hair, the color of ravens, is long on the top, cropped close on the sides, and looks like it's had fingers and wind running through it all morning. Dark aviator sunglasses grace his nose, but that's all I can manage from his profile. I can't see his face from where I stand yards away in the parking lot, becoming a shadow, blending in.

I'm good at blending in, and disappearing from view.

Maybe he's a teacher? Could that be why he's here so early? I'm here as the sun comes up so that I can get a lay of the land before the school day chaos ensues.

But just as the thought of him possibly being a teacher enters my brain, it goes right back out the window. A giggling, gangly, half-naked girl dismounts from the passenger seat. She runs around the front of the car, meeting him, sidling up to his strong figure like a cat purring in heat.

And that's when I spot the varsity jacket slung over the headrest of the driver's seat. No, he's not a teacher.

He's a jock.

I should have known, but I wasn't used to this breed of high school male, so my radar was off. Where I came from, druggies were popular and that was giving them too much credit. Most of the kids at my school in Florida flunked out before sophomore year, and the sports teams were, essentially, a joke.

But this guy, he's got popular bad boy written all over him.

And it's too early for them to be here, because surely these beautiful people don't need to study. And he is definitely not the type to show up for a before school detention, even if he was penalized with one.

I watch them, still undetected, as they slink into a glass-paneled side door, the girl swiveling her head right before they pop inside just to see if they've been caught.

Maybe it's the pause between songs, or the empty parking lot, or the sun beating down on my back.

But I realize I'm utterly alone, and this mystery has presented itself. What are they doing? Why are they here?

The suspense novel reader and writer in me has to know.

I follow them, unplugging my earbuds and rolling the chord up, sticking them in my back pocket.

The door they went in is off the parking lot; I should be headed toward the front entrance doors around the other side of the building. My heart is beating, and I can't get the sight of that boy rumbling up in his open top Jeep out of my head.

I feel like a peeping Tom, but this is nothing new. One of my favorite activities back home in Florida was people watching. At school, at my job at the local bait and tackle shop, in the mall, walking around the beach. Watching people and their actions or interactions was immensely interesting to me. Human behavior, people trying to appear a certain way or hiding something ... I was nothing if not a sucker for secrets.

I creep to the door, careful because if they're right on the other side, they'll see me. I press my body up against the brick exterior of the building, and slowly turn my head to the right to look through the door.

The door is an exit to one of the stairwells in the school, and I can see through to the brightly lit corridor through the door opposite the one I'm peeking in. Out of the corner of my eye I see movement right before the stairs, which sit on the far side of the room I'm looking into.

And there, leaning against the wall, is the bad boy. His head tilted back, eyes closed, hands thrust into a head of hair.

A head of hair from the girl who is kneeling in front of him, giving him a blow job.

My heart starts with a shock, pumping faster and faster like it might just jump out of my throat at any moment. I was already sweating because of the walk and humidity, but my shirt starts sticking to my skin, every part of me flushing.

There they are, in the school building at six thirty, having oral sex. I'm shocked, although I've seen things more lewd than this growing up where I did. I'm not sure why I feel like a raw nerve right now, but it's something in his expression.

Primal. Pure satisfaction. Dirty secrets in the stairwell of a school.

It's all so forbidden, especially to my virgin heart. And thighs.

I must be breathing too hard on the glass, my breaths coming out in puffs, because just then, his head comes down from where it's pressed up against the wall.

He looks forward, and our eyes connect.

Green, the color of glittering stones. They contain every single bad, dirty wish that takes a good girl down. That can get her on her back, out of her clothes.

Those eyes are potent, and I shouldn't look into them for fear of paralysis. For fear of falling. For fear of wanting something that a boy like that could never promise me.

I look into those eyes, and then down to the lips.

Which are smiling a Cheshire cat grin.

3

CAIN

A doe in headlights, like the ones my father had shot or run over and hung around his den.

Those baby blues and white-blond hair were virginal, everything about her rings out as pure. Except for the rack she's attempting to hide under that T-shirt. Those are more than a handful each, and my cock stirs in Christy's mouth as I stare at the voyeur on the other side of the glass.

Her eyes are saucers, rimmed by thick black lashes obviously enhanced with makeup, even if it is the only stitch of it she has on. The rest of her face is bare, her lips natural, her skin a shade of sun-tanned freckles. She watches as I get head, the girl on her knees in front of me cupping my balls and slicking her tongue down my shaft.

Her fingers touch those nude lips, and I see it, a twitch of her left knee. She's getting turned on.

I groan, because it feels too damn good, and raise an eyebrow, watching her watch me.

Who is she? Maybe a freshman, I'd never seen her before. This school is too big for me to know everyone, even though everyone knows me. I also wasn't into learning about others. My popularity drew the slutty or cool ones to me, and that's all I had to do to make a friend or get a girl.

But I'm not naïve. These people were clingers, hangers-on. They all want a piece of me so they could say that they knew Cain Kent when I finally made it to the big time football league.

Kelly, or Nelly? Damn, I already forgot her name. She was sucking on my cock and I'd forgotten her name.

We'd met at the weekly bonfire party on Saturday and had drunkenly talked about sneaking into school for a hot make out session. So we'd waited until Monday, to make it realistic, and here we were. In the stairwell, her lips suctioned to my dick, and I was close to coming even before I knew that this mysterious fairy of a girl was being a voyeur on my pleasure.

When I glance back up, after watching pulling Kelly or Nelly's hair to maneuver her head the way I want, she's gone.

Cupping the mouth at my balls with both hands, I fuck her mouth in a dirty, rough way. The novelty of being at school was wearing off, and I was hungry as shit. I just wanted to come and then go to the diner for a massive breakfast sandwich.

My spine begins to tingle and my knees lock up, my body rigid. I see the wisps of fireworks at the corners of my eyes as I let go, spilling my seed into her pretty mouth.

"Thanks, darlin'," I drawl as I zip up my shorts, moving away from her without a backward glance.

Hell, I don't even offer her a hand up to get off of her knees. And I'm definitely not going to give her a ride back to wherever she needed to go.

Walking out to the sounds of her hesitant protest, I jump into my doorless Jeep and start the engine, turning the volume on the Florida Georgia Line song all the way up.

Peeling out of the parking lot, I let the morning sun wash over my face.

Head, loud music and a greasy breakfast sandwich all before seven a.m.? Could my teenage life be any more idyllic?

Nah, it couldn't. Mostly everything came easy to me and I took full advantage of it. I don't mean to sound like a cocky little prick, but when your life played out like a movie, it was hard not to.

I drive through town, stopping for my sandwich at Hendrick's Deli, on the house because I'm Cain Kent.

There is still an hour until I need to be back at school, perks of having a free period for the first block of the day. So I drive out to my favorite spot, three miles out of Haven and on the shores of McCray Lake. Throwing my Jeep into park, I watch the sun rise over the water and eat my breakfast, the post-come feeling still tingling in my veins.

Yeah, life is pretty damn good in my neck of the woods.

But, as soon as I thought this, and it was happening often enough now to unsettle me, anxiety rippled through my stomach like someone petting a dog's hair the wrong way.

This was my last year in Haven. After I graduated, life became real. College football meant serious business, hundreds more plays to memorize, keeping up a grade point average while traveling the country.

I was already committed to the best football school of them all, the big bad school in Austin, so I wouldn't be going far. When I signed my commitment I was told I'd be their starting quarterback, no redshirting. But, of course, there are no guarantees.

It was a huge weight of pressure on my shoulders. Of course, I wanted football to be my career, but here in Haven, it was easy. Everyone already knew how good I was, there was no proving a thing. Girls understood their place in my world; ornaments and sex objects, as bad as that sounded. I didn't have time for anything else. My friends were my boys forever, and I knew the lay of the land.

Next year, I'd be a small fish in a huge pond. My entire life, I'd been the shit. The king.

I get out, loving the smell of the long grass and muddy water. Looking out over the lake, home of summer day drinking and nights of cars parked, steamy windows; I smile.

I had less than one year left. I'd better make the most of it.

4

HARPER

I'd planned to get to school early.

To walk the halls and find my scheduled rooms and then walk them again to get the timing down.

I was nothing if not type A.

What I didn't expect was to view the full-frontal peep show before I even entered the building.

It had thrown my entire day off, and I felt flushed and discombobulated still, three periods into the day.

Math was my most challenging subject, and it wasn't ideal that it was my first class each day. I considered myself a good student, but put numbers in front of me and I couldn't compute. Add in my morning's excitement and trigonometry was impossible.

Second period was an elective class, and I'd chosen photography thinking that it would be interesting but also easy. Turns out, the teacher was a former Texas beauty queen who knew more about posing for pictures instead of lenses and shutter speeds. I rolled my eyes no less than fifteen times.

Not to mention that Haven High school was completely different than any place I'd ever been. There were girls walking around in high heels. Heels ... in high school. I was lucky if my classmates in Florida even wore shoes in the morning, coming right off the beach after catching swells.

It was like a runway in this building, girls with highlighted, blown out hair. Midriff baring tops, boys with bodies like I'd never even dreamed. Football jerseys and cheerleading uniforms everywhere. And the air ... it was different. Ripe with cliques and privilege, I'd only read about schools like this in books.

I felt completely underdressed in my ripped skinny jeans, not done on purpose or by design, and plain beige T-shirt. My hair, white-blond and straight, hung long down my back, but there was nothing special about it. And aside from mascara, I didn't bother with makeup. If I didn't coat the black ink on my lashes, I'd look albino with my pale eyelashes.

But it was time for honors English, and I was in my element and ready for books. Reading took me to another plane, and hopefully we'd have some creative writing time in class for me to work on my own novel that I was slowly but surely getting done. Since I'd picked up my first Judy Blume book, I'd known that an author was what I wanted to be when I grew up. I figured that college was a long shot with the amount of money we already didn't have, so I'd just start self-publishing and see what happened. I'd been researching for years, taking free writing seminars at the community college in Florida that they offered to high school students, and teaching myself graphic editing programs to make covers. This was my dream, my quiet dream, and after four years, I was close to making it come true. Nothing could deter me.

I'm busy setting my textbooks out and grabbing a pen out of my backpack as the other students walk in, chattering away. I picked a desk in the second row, toward the outside of the classroom. It was unassuming, just like I was trying to be. As the new girl, I was nearly invisible, which was all right with me.

And then the only roadblock that could possibly knock me off course walked in.

Green eyes had a different girl than this morning draped around his arm, and a guy in a football jersey was walking next to them, talking loudly with his hands.

They didn't spot me, didn't even bother looking at anyone, though everyone else was openly staring at them. I imagined it was what celebrities must be like.

They sit in the back row, horsing around. I wonder how he even made it into a class like this, although it's possible that whatever those kinds of kids want, they get.

"You might want to pick your jaw up." A voice comes from just behind me.

I turn, seeing the pretty redhead chewing a pale blue fingernail.

"Sorry?" I can feel the blush creeping up my cheeks.

"The Alphas. They're glittering, I get it, but I wouldn't get mixed up in that."

I'm confused, as she's wearing a cheerleading uniform just like the rest of the pretty, popular girls I've seen sauntering around the halls so far.

The longer I look at her, the more I see how attractive she really is. Her features are delicate, her hair long and curly in a perfectly unruly way, and she's toned. The kind of toned you see in a magazine and know you'll never be.

"Don't get swept up in all that. Especially as a new kid. Better to just do your own thing." She swipes a curtain of scarlet over her shoulder.

I can't tell if she's giving me friendly advice or warning me off. "How did you know that I was new?"

It was late September, so it wasn't a far off assumption that someone showing up in your class who hadn't been there since the start of the school year was new. But, I was trying to fly under the radar and so I didn't need the whole front of the class introduction.

The cheerleader gives me a *duh* look. "It's almost October. You've never been in my honors English class before, and I've never seen you. I'm Mary-Kate, by the way."

I can't tell if she's pulling my leg by talking to me, but her southern twang is inviting and I don't know a soul here. So I bite.

"Harper Posy, resident new kid. Thanks for the ... tip?"

She nods her head. "Welcome. Seriously, don't get wrapped up in the drama here. There is way too much of it."

"Says the cheerleader." I snort.

"New girl has sarcasm, I like it." She grins. "I cheer because I like it, and do you know the kind of college scholarships I can get?"

I never considered this, but I'm sure sports bring in some money. Too bad I had no eye-hand coordination, and my talents were best left to words and stories.

"Your initials are HP? That's sick." Mary-Kate giggles, and I don't find her observation annoying.

Like I normally do. You can't grow up in the English speaking world and not be teased if your initials are the same as a fictional wizard that the entire planet is obsessed with. My mother included, which is why she named me Harper Pearl Posy. Technically, my initials are HPP, but those who teased me growing up never seemed to care about that. I'd always wished that my mom and dad had gotten married, or that Dad had fought harder for my last name to be his own, Baker. At least then I wouldn't have these initials, or have been teased in grade school during the song, "*Ring Around the Rosie*."

I don't get a chance to answer her, because class starts just then. The teacher comes in, an older man with a graying goatee and woven bracelets, and I instantly take a liking to him. He's like a hybrid hippie with his unkempt hair and cowboy boots, and I feel like this is exactly what a good English teacher should look like.

"I'd like to mention that we have a new student with us.

You don't have to call me Mr. Whethers, just call me Todd. This class is an open discussion on books, not some bullshit forty minutes trying to look for symbolism that isn't there."

Thank God. This class is going to be awesome. My solace in this wacky school.

Just as Todd is about to launch into a list of books we're expected to prepare for each week, I hear a ringtone go off in the back of the class.

We all look back, and I hear Todd sigh. "Look, while I'm a lenient teacher, don't abuse that power I'm putting in your hands."

And as he's saying this, the guy I saw in the hallway this morning, starts to FaceTime with someone on the other end.

"Hey, bro, what's up?" He holds the phone up and waves hi to the person on the other end of the camera.

And that's enough for me. I've had a stressful morning, due in part to him and his sex acts. I've been running around this school like a mad woman. And now, in my favorite subject, he's interrupting by being a jackass.

"I know that you must think the world revolves around you, whoever you are, and that you don't have to try in school because who cares if you become the next guy behind the counter pouring slushies. But you're being a total asshole right now. Have some respect, put your phone down, and pay attention. Because unlike you, some of us enjoy school, and actually want to excel at it so that we can go on to do bigger things."

5

HARPER

The entire classroom is so silent, you could hear a pin drop.

"Um, excuse me?" One of the ditzy girls next to him turns an evil eye on me.

In my fit of rage, I can feel that my face has become hot, and it's probably bright red. The whole room is staring at me, including Mr. Green Eyes.

And he's wearing a shit-eating grin on those full lips. "Cain Kent."

He clicks his call closed and gives me his full attention. I'm so annoyed that I don't even care if I'm having an outburst. I'm usually the kind of girl who doesn't want to be seen or heard, but I've had enough.

"What?" I seethe, annoyed.

He levels me with his intense gaze, the air around him moving for his big ego. "That's my name. You should know the name of the guy you're calling out. Big mistake, by the way."

Out of the corner of my eye, Mary-Kate is waving her finger across her neck, as if to tell me to abort my suicide mission.

Todd seems to sense the tension, because he clears his

throat. "We have enough drama with Shakespeare, folks. Let's focus on the lesson."

I glare one last time before I turn in my seat, smiling apologetically at my teacher.

The class goes by in a blur as my nerves calm down, and I'm actually really excited for the books he has planned. He belongs in a liberal arts college, but I'm happy that Todd is here instead.

The bell rings and the classroom begins to empty out, and I see Mary-Kate idling as I collect my things, checking my schedule and the number of the classroom I need to sprint to next.

Cain Kent, or hot jackass as I am now referring to him in my head, passes me. His stare is hot and uncomfortable, and I try not to squirm.

"See you around, Peep."

Oh. My. God.

All of my insides flush, because I know why he just called me that. Short for Peeping Tom. He saw me this morning, watching him, and he remembered. Shit.

"Girl, I don't know what size balls you have, but they must be brass because you just picked a fight with the biggest bull of the bunch." Mary-Kate whistles as Cain walks out.

"What is that guy's problem?" I shrug, annoyed.

"That *guy* is Cain Kent. Superstar quarterback. Most popular guy in school. All around jerk but hot as Hades. He is the guy that teenage girls have wet dreams over. If you're trying to make waves as the new girl, you just got your wish."

My stomach drops out just a little, because that wasn't my intention. I just wanted to submerse myself in English class, not become the apple of some douchebags beautiful green eyes.

"Whatever, I'm not worried about Cain Kent. I'm here to do well and graduate." We walk together out of class and down the hall.

"Sounds like a plan to me. I think I like your style, Harper. When do you have lunch?" Her cheer uniform garners a lot of waves and hellos as we walk.

I look at my schedule. "Um, fifth period."

"Me too. Come find me, I usually sit in the senior courtyard, out the big window doors in the cafeteria."

I have to look at her, because it's hard to understand why she's being so nice. So I ask her. "Why are you being so nice?"

She shrugs, and I can sense her easy nature. "Because new people are interesting. Because I like the color of your hair or the fact that you just told off the biggest man on campus. Mostly, I'm just bored of all of these morons around here. So let's be friends."

I take this into consideration, and decide that maybe I want a friend. I've never really been a "friends" type of girl; In Florida, I mostly just kept to myself, read, wrote and worked if I wasn't at school. I didn't really need a lot of interaction ... I guess I was a self-sufficient introvert in that way.

But something about Mary-Kate connects with me, and I nod. "Okay, I'll come find you during lunch."

I wander into the cafeteria for fifth period, staring up at the vaulted ceilings and then down the line of food options. It wasn't a five-star restaurant, but it was a hell of a lot better than what I'd had at my high school in the Keys. There was a vegetarian station, a whole line for barbecued meats, and even a wok station with chicken lo mein that smelled half decent.

And the students ... you could damn near drown in how many people packed this massive space. Before, I'd gone to school where the average graduating class size was about three hundred, and maybe a third of those people actually showed up to school each day.

At Haven, there were about seven hundred kids in each grade. And none of them missed ... or so it seemed from the amount of bodies I had to plow through in the halls. No one went off campus for lunch either, I assumed, since benches and benches of lunch tables were packed with eating, gossiping, laughing high school students.

I finally found the senior courtyard that Mary-Kate had told me about earlier, and pushed through the doors. My stomach rumbled as I did, and I realized that I'd been too nervous to eat breakfast, and had forgotten about the granola bar I'd zipped in the front part of my backpack.

Oh yeah, I forgot to mention the backpack. Apparently, Jansport was a no-go at this school. Almost every girl in the place carried a large tote bag in either leather or a colorful print. I was like a fish swimming upstream, the uncool stream that is, with my navy blue backpack.

Looking around, I take in the enclosed eating area. It's essentially a brick patio wedged between the open square two of the wings of the building formed. There are a handful of students out here, and about ten or so picnic tables.

"Harper!" Mary-Kate waves at me from a table farther away from the entrance back into the school.

I walk toward her, and see two other girls, one in a cheerleading uniform and one in plainclothes, sitting with her.

"Ladies, this is Harper," she introduces me as I walk up, and I feel awkward taking a seat but do it anyway.

"Hi, I'm Tisha." The girl in the uniform gives me a once over.

The one in plainclothes is a little nicer, sticking her hand out for me to shake. "Hey, I'm Imogen. I really like your earrings."

Touching my lobes and feeling my mother's borrowed sapphire studs there, I smile. "Thanks. Nice to meet you both."

I take out my granola bar, too anxious to go in and try to figure out the lunch lines, and scarf it down. Mary-Kate starts talking, rambling on about this or that going on at school, what she's wearing to the homecoming dance in two weeks and more of the typical high school gossip.

"So, you're the new girl?" A sharp voice comes from behind me.

I turn, shielding my eyes from the sun beating down on the courtyard. A girl stands there, but really, she's more like a woman. Curvy and tan, with hair out of a Pantene commercial and teeth so brilliantly white they'd definitely pass the tissue test, she looks like she belongs on a pageant stage.

"Um ..." There are two girls flanking her, all three of them in cheerleading uniforms, and they're definitely looking at me like I'm a threat.

Mary-Kate steps in. "Annabelle, hey!"

I've only known her for a couple of hours, but I can tell that my new friend's voice is way too high. This girl intimidates her, which I didn't think was really possible.

"MK." She nods at her, almost like she's putting her in her place. "I don't believe your new friend has been introduced to me."

As if she can't just speak for herself? Who is this girl, Beyoncé?

"Harper, this is Annabelle Mills, captain of the cheer squad." There is something Mary-Kate isn't saying, but it's implied.

This girl is the head honcho. The queen bee. The girl all other girls at this school both emulate and fear. There is one in every town, and it looks like I just stepped on her nest, and she's pissed.

"That's right." Annabelle bends down, looking at me like a child who needs to be dealt with. "And I've been hearing an awful lot about you in the short time you've been at my school.

My school, got that? I say who is and isn't in. I fill these halls with what everyone should be talking about, and with your little stunt this morning, you're now the talk of the town. I don't like that. You don't want me not to like that, Harper, I promise."

My hackles were rising, and while I wanted to tell her to fuck off, I also didn't want to draw any more attention to myself. I could care less about this high school and it's cliques. The more anonymous I could stay, the better. So, I simply nodded. "Got it."

She straightened, smiling a smile that could curdle milk. "Good."

Annabelle snapped her fingers, turned on her heels, and the two girls with her raced to the double doors to let her back in the building. I kid you not, they opened the doors for her like she was unable to touch a door handle.

Just before she was about to stride back into the school, she turned. "Oh, and Harper?"

I was still staring at her, hadn't stopped since she came out here to challenge me. "Yes?"

"Don't even think about going near Cain. He is mine."

6

CAIN

The locker room smells like sweat and dirty football equipment, but to me, it is the scent of my life.

It is the aroma of victory, of my future, of a Friday night well spent.

Of course, today is only practice. We have a game in five days, and Monday practices after school were typically the easiest. Drills, working out plays that had failed in last week's game, sometimes film.

But we were deeper into the season, and this game meant more this week. So I knew we were in for some hell.

That was fine, I worked best under insults and doubts.

As usual, my teammates are gossiping, calling each other pussies, and boasting about which girl they were going to bang this weekend.

"So, Kent, got girl number ten lined up?" Josiah, the second string running back, asks.

My mind flashes back to innocent blue eyes, and a biting, harsh mouth. The way she challenged me, whatever her name was ... it has me interested. Girls in Haven ... hell, girls I'd encountered anywhere, didn't challenge me. They fell at my feet, or on their knees to get dick-level. They swooned, acted interested in my football stats while toying with my arm muscles, tried to take their shirts off during games of beer pong.

But school me on class manners and English lit? No, they most certainly didn't do that.

"There are a few possibilities in my line of sight." I smirk a cocky grin.

I could win easily, bag any football groupie or dumb freshman at a bonfire as soon as this weekend. But for the same twisted, sick reason that I was playing this game, I wanted the final score to be ... meaningful.

Not in a, fall in love type of way. Fuck that shit. No, I want the tenth girl to be a conquest. I wanted to slay a dragon, hook a big fish.

"I bet Kent can't get that tenth girl to sleep with him before Christmas break." Grady, our defensive end, one of my best friends and another contestant in the race to ten girls, throws his pads over his head and begins to strap them on.

"We're already in the middle of a bet. No side bets. Plus, you really want me to beat your ass that quickly?" I lace up a cleat and grab my helmet from a bench.

Grady smirks, his blond hair running long down his bulked up neck. "You're just threatened that I might beat you."

I snicker. "Yeah, right. What number girl are you on, six? And with your jacked up dick, there is no way you'll convince four more girls to sleep with you by June."

"You never know, crazier things have happened." Will, a cornerback and another guy in on the competition, gives his input.

Will is in last place with three girls, and I know he has no intention of winning. He fell for the third girl he slept with and they've been together since. Even though we technically still count him as one of the six, we know he'd never cheat on Lynn to win a bet.

"Yeah, crazy things like you falling in love. Pussy." Emmit, another player in on the competition, walks by in full gear.

Emmit, Grady, Will, Paul and Joshua, and I were competing for bragging rights and the key to The Atrium as well.

Ah, the key to The Atrium. Complete solitude in one of the creepiest, and coolest places in Haven. The ability to own it, to throw a party whenever you felt like it.

Not like I didn't already have an entire house at my disposal. That's what you got for being an army brat.

My mind wanders back to the girl in question, the one I was considering for number ten.

I still hadn't gotten her name, but fuck if her face while she'd been yelling at me wasn't burned into my memory. All that light hair, that freckled skin. Pure innocence, waiting to be ruined.

Was I sick? Probably. Was I an asshole? Definitely. The therapist my dad had taken me to in elementary school had warned us both that my mother abandoning us could cause commitment phobia and anger issues when it came to women, both in a relationship and authority sense. Guess that guy with the million degrees was right, although I don't think you need a masters to determine that.

My mother had up and took off when I was six, not that I remember much of it. Or her.

Whatever, my anger and ego is just who I am. And girlfriends aren't something I am interested in anyway. Sex, that's what I am after.

And hopefully, Little Miss Virgin will comply.

As if Grady can read my mind, he speaks up. "Cain isn't going to win. Not when random new girls are calling him out in class. What's with that chick, man?"

My gut roils in annoyance. She tried to embarrass me. *Me.*

"Man, fuck that girl. If she thinks she's going to gain her five minutes of fame here by challenging me, she's got another thing coming."

"I heard she's pretty hot." Emmitt laces up his black uniform pants, the twinkle in his weirdly purple eyes mischievous.

"Yeah, like some kind of sexy fairy or some shit. I saw her sitting in the senior courtyard at lunch with MK, she's got a big rack for her body."

"We talking C's or D's?" Emmitt asks.

Josiah taps a finger to his chin. "I'd say C's, but they look fucking huge because she's pretty small."

"All the better to pick a girl up. Maybe I'll add her to my competition list." Grady winks at me.

Something in me rolls, a wave of raw instinct telling me to say, "No one adds her to their list. That one is mine to bang if I even want her."

Will gives me a strange look. "Sounds like you want her, man."

We have an all-pads practice today, and our conversation ceases when one of the assistant coaches yells at us to get our pansy asses out on the field.

I walk out of the locker room, the gold and black colors of our school painted over every inch. Football in Texas is an industry, and in Haven, it's no different. Our facilities are state of the art, and after winning State last year, we got some big donor money from some of the richer families in town, and in the county. Our sport was a religion in this neck of the woods, and people worship accordingly.

It was a blessing and a curse, being held in that high of a regard. Most of the time, I felt like a damn god or something. But the pressure, it could fuck with your head. Especially as the one player that always got blamed if we lost. I constantly felt like I was on a hamster wheel; I had to keep moving in order to power the world.

Luckily, though, football was a genetic part of me. My father often said I came out of the womb trying to read a playbook. As a kid, he said that instead of playing video games or playing hide and seek, I was drawing up routes and using my stuffed animals to execute them.

I love football like I love breathing. It is a part of me, and since I can remember, I'd thought like a quarterback.

"All right, men. We're running offensive plays today. I want every pass play in the book fucking memorized. We're six and oh, and if you think I'm going to lose my hundredth game, you're fucking wrong!"

Our head coach, David Nichols, is yelling already and it's only Monday. We have a game on Friday against one of the better teams in the conference, and none of us want to lose, obviously. But especially not Coach Nichols. It will be his hundredth win as head coach at Haven, and while he's a damn stickler, he's also a damn good coach. I'm lucky that I don't have one of those abusive assholes I've heard about. He works us hard, but he also praises and teaches.

The sun beats down on the turf, and the light from the bleachers almost blinds me. My muscles rev like an idling engine, and the red pinny I have on over my black uniform says I'm off limits. My right arm, my throwing arm, flexes and tenses, so ready to get out there.

In no time, my offensive unit is on the field, all of the guys looking to me for direction. The play maker, the brains of the operation, that's what I am. I relish it, being the head honcho, and my mind is a steel trap when it comes to memorizing plays.

After huddling and explaining the play in as little terms possible, because we have to think of this as a game scenario and the clock running down, we clap our hands and get in formation.

Sweat trickles down my forehead under my helmet, and even though I know I won't get hit, I prepare as if I might. One of my Pop Warner coaches once told me that the best players have talent, yes, but the work they put in is more important. That if you treat every second of every practice exactly like it's the most important game of your life, then there will be no way that any player will ever be better than you.

And that's what I try to do every single time I step out onto this field.

The line bends down, the ball is placed in my center's hands, and "Haven Black seventy, Haven Black seventy, hut, hut!"

Things start to shift, the defensive line begins to blitz, and I shrug out of the way, sidestepping like I'm a champion ballroom dancer. Light on his feet, that's what all the papers say about me.

I read the defense and assess my receivers running down the field. Split-second decisions and an arm like a goddamn NASA rocket, that's my job.

Emmitt is sprinting down the field, his wide receiver body tall and lean as he cuts his route and escapes coverage.

Something in my head clicks, I've come to think of it as the "go signal." I can't describe it, have never told anyone about it, but there is this ... maybe a chime that goes off in my brain at the exact moment that I should throw the ball. Each time it happens, I let it fly, and I know it will land perfectly in a pair of my teammates hands, ensuring a touchdown.

And so, I let it fly, putting the perfect spiral on the ball aimed directly for Emmitt.

I don't have to watch it arc, or here the applause and whoops from my coaches and teammates, to know that it landed exactly where I wanted it to. Does that make me cocky? Yes.

But when you have talent and hard work, no player on the field is going to be better than you.

7

HARPER

Working in a bait and tackle shop while I lived in Florida had happened by accident.

I don't particularly like fishing, I'd rather sit on a boat and read a good book than stare at a pole in the water. But when I'd been looked for a job my sophomore year of high school, the guy Mom had been dating at the time liked to catch trout, and was friendly with the owner of the store he bought supplies at.

Turns out, my relationship with the Warrens, the owners of Keys Bait and Tackle, lasted far longer than that moron's date-span with Mom. But hey, I was thankful for the job.

It had been an easy, relatively safe job working behind the counter and assisting in finding specific products.

When we arrived in Texas, I knew that both Mom and I would have to find jobs. While we weren't paying rent at my grandmother's, or so I thought, I knew we had little to no money. Mom needed to find a teaching job, or somewhere that would hire her quickly, to begin saving. I didn't know what her end game was, if she planned to stay here or move on after I graduated.

And me ... I needed my "get out" money. I'd been saving slowly but surely since sophomore year, and I had two thousand dollars put aside for my next chapter. It didn't sound like much, but it was enough for a plane ticket, and hopefully I could self-publish my book by the end of this school year and begin making royalties off of that. All I had to do was have enough after that for a cheap place wherever I decided to go.

Italy.

London.

Bali.

Hawaii.

I'd debated all of these places, or other quiet corners of the world where it would be just me and my computer, me and my words. I'd lived with next to nothing for my entire life, so the nomad lifestyle wouldn't bother me one bit. I loved my mom, but I'd always felt like I belonged somewhere else. Like there was this entire world out there and I'd never seen any of it. Even at my young age of seventeen, I felt the tug to go elsewhere.

So when Grandma had surprisingly come to me in the living room two days ago, saying she had a job lined up for me, I'd jumped at the chance.

"I'm told that you worked at a fishing supply shop in Florida." Her curt tone was no-nonsense, all the time.

I'd been writing, and I looked up from the keyboard. "I did, yeah."

"I've gotten you a job at the local bait, tackle and hunting shop. You have an interview on Thursday after school, although it's a formality."

I was surprised, but happy to have a job without having to really work for it. "Thanks, Grandma."

She nodded, and I swear she smiled. "Everyone works when they live under this roof, minors included. You'll also be expected to do some minimal farm work for the time your mother decides to set her bags in Haven."

Her voice is bitter, and I know that she thinks my mother is frivolous and spontaneous. And she is, but it's what makes me love her.

"She means well. She's been a good parent." I sound like the mother in our duo.

"And the fact that you have the awareness to understand that is sad. You're just a girl." My grandma frowns. "But, you seem like a hard worker, and I appreciate that."

That was basically her telling me she loved me, in her own weird way.

The exchange had been strange, and sad. Did she regret not accepting my mother for what she was? She was almost certainly disappointed in her, but I could also tell with each new conversation we had, that she regretted losing so much time with the only family she had left.

I walk out of the tackle shop carrying a polo shirt with the Hook & Hunt logo on it, and a printed weekly schedule of my hours. My new boss, Bob Custer, is a nice, if not gruff, man who seems like he'll be fine to work with if I just do my job.

The store is located on Haven's Main Street, which is home to the typical Main Street kind of stores. A butcher, a post office, library, coffee shop, dry cleaners, and a diner. No name brands, and there was a bookstore that I definitely needed to check out. The sign in the window said they had used copies, and I bet there were some gems among those stacks.

We'd been here almost a week, and I would be lying if I said Texas wasn't growing on me. It had a charm about it. I loved that when I walked past the bar on Main Street, Dolly Parton's voice drifted out onto the sidewalk from the speakers inside. I loved sitting out in the fields at my grandma's house, as was my nightly routine now. I'd find different pastures, and the other night I'd even spied a few of the horses that had wandered to the back part of her property. School was still a tornado of trendy clothing and the popular crowd, but my classes were good and the teachers here actually cared whether their students graduated.

"Hey, Peep, wait up."

I hear the voice from behind me, and although I've only heard it a few times now, I know who is going to be advancing on me.

My heart rate spikes, but I keep walking, my flip-flops slapping the pavement.

"Now that's rude, ignoring a friend's request." Cain Kent runs around the side of me, and cuts my movement off as his body stands in front of mine like a road block.

"We're not friends." I look up at him, his height reaching about a foot above my own, and scowl.

It's difficult not to stare at a boy like Cain. His looks are like a storm cloud, dark and harsh, captivating, but beautiful in their doom.

We must look like complete opposites standing here, on this stretch of sidewalk. Him, dark and foreboding, and me, light and naïve like a doe.

"We could be. I can be real friendly, Harper Posy." His mouth tips up, and I see the small silver scar on his chin stretch, marking the olive tone of his skin. "Yeah, I can find out any answer to any question I have about you without going to the source. Remember that."

"Oh, I think we both know how friendly you can be." I raise an eyebrow, trying to hide my own shock that those words just came out of my mouth.

In the week we've been in English together, I haven't said any more to him. And he hasn't acknowledged my presence. At first, it felt like he was purposely ignoring me, and that annoyed me. But then I thought, why should I care?

And now here he is, trying to get in my pants in front of the dry cleaners.

Cain's clover-colored eyes twinkle. "Mm, so you like what you saw."

"No, but you should probably tell your girlfriend that another girl was ... pleasuring you just hours before she accosted me."

His beautiful face screws up. "My girlfriend?"

I scuff my sneaker into the sidewalk. I don't know the politics around here, can't navigate them. It's like I left Florida and stepped into a world that spoke a completely different language. People say Florida is its own country, but Texas is a whole other beast unto itself.

"Annabelle Mills ... she told me to stay away from you. Maybe you should let her know that I'm not the one she has to worry about. Or do you treat all of them like your girlfriend?" I sneer, disgusted with him.

Not only was he dirty, sneaking into school to get a blow job, he was a cheater on top of it.

Cain laughs, the sound like melted butter on my skin. "Annabelle is not my girlfriend. I don't do girlfriends. And even if I did, Annabelle would definitely not be one of them."

Now I feel like an idiot, because the mean girl tricked me into being intimidated. Or even caring that she was someone to Cain.

His attractiveness threw me off, made me weak and dumb. I had never felt this way before, and it made me feel even dumber. I was actually mad at myself that I couldn't fully focus in his presence.

"But you know, you seem like a boyfriend type of girl. Let me show you how fun having no strings attached can be." He moves closer, and I can smell the dirt and grass on the Haven Football T-shirt he's wearing.

I step back, pissed that he knows he's getting under my skin. "Listen, *buddy*. I'm not any type of girl that you've ever encountered. I don't want a boyfriend, and I also don't want to ride the town jock. Leave me alone."

Flames, green and angry, ignite in his pupils. But he chuckles, disguising it. "Oh, *new girl* ... you actually think I want to fuck you? *You*? Don't make me laugh."

He calls me by the name as an insult, like he won't call me my real name because it's too polite.

Cain is just inches away from me now, his head tilted down so that our lips are lined up. The electricity between us is palpable, and it's traitorous for my heart to be doing what it's doing. And at the same time, my cheeks burn with shame. With embarrassment that he just knocked me down ten pegs.

His big body is too close, and he walks me backward into the brick exterior of the building. "You're a toy, a play thing. Something to taunt, not stick my cock in. Believe me, I have girls at that school lining up for that. I can leave you alone, but I know that after you've had me this close, you won't be able to sleep without thinking of what's underneath these clothes."

Cain Kent points to himself, and I hate that my breath is coming out in puffs.

Just as abruptly as he stopped me, he turns on his heel and leaves. No backward glances.

8

CAIN

"Hey, old man." I hold my phone up, making sure my face comes into view.

"Who you calling 'old man'? I'll have you know that I just re-programed a computer in under an hour as one of my training tasks for this mission."

I smile, because really, my dad is the farthest thing from old. As a general in the army, he's one the smartest, bravest guys I know. And luckily for me, he's also a good father, even though his job and his broken heart keep him halfway across the world most days. But, he's always been supportive, and isn't one of those prick fathers who teaches with his hands or thinks that because he's in the military, it's okay to be cold and punishing.

Nah, my dad is pretty cool. He just ... wasn't around much. We talked a lot on FaceTime, sent emails, and he watched my games via the Internet.

"How's it looking for the game tonight?" Dad is in a white tee and the wall behind him looks to be made of straight drywall.

He's somewhere in Korea, although he can't specifically tell me where.

"Marshall High doesn't have a chance, we're going to smoke them. We've been running some new pass plays with a slant route, and they've been going really well in practice."

Dad nods as another soldier walks behind him with a gun strapped to his back. "Awesome, you looked great last week. Just keep those feet steady, no going twinkle toes."

We both laugh at the inside joke. When I was a kid, and my family was still intact and neither of my parents had run from the other, Dad was all about helping me excel at football. Not in a pressuring way, but because he knew I loved it.

My dad and my grandfather are the only people in my life who I allow myself to be vulnerable with. They know the real me, the guy underneath the cocky prick façade or behind the quarterback arm that people tended to see before the person.

"How is it over there?" I was always cautious to ask.

It wasn't like he was going to give me the real answer anyway. "It's okay, missions are going as planned. Only eight more months, bud, I'll be home right in time for graduation."

I nod, a bitter taste filling my mouth. It wasn't like he had to go, he had enough years and missions to retire with a nice fat pension and the ability to get some teaching or training job at the local military base. But we both knew he would never stop. He couldn't stand to be in Haven. We stayed because the football team was so great, and from the time I was little, we both knew that I was going to try to get to the national league. Going to Haven High School gave me a better chance to score a scholarship at a top college, and from there drawing interest from big time scouts to get drafted.

Dad sacrificed for me, because he'd rather be in hell on hearth than in Haven. It was where he and my mom had fallen in love, where they'd had me, and eventually, where she'd left him. I don't know the full details, to his credit he never tried to poison me against her. But I knew that being here, in our house and in town, was painful for him.

So he kept taking tours, even if it meant he couldn't be here for me.

"Can't wait, we can go see Brett Eldridge, too. He's going to play a concert at that outdoor stadium like, two weeks after graduation." I'd already been eyeing tickets. "Maybe we can take Gramps."

Dad nods, but I can see it in his eyes. Most likely, we were never taking Gramps out of the nursing home for a concert. Church on Sunday was the only trip he could muster the energy for.

"All right, son, I have to go. Tell your grandpa I say hi when you see him on Monday. Talk soon, love you, kid."

"Love you, Dad."

And then the phone went dark with the ending of the call. I always told him I loved him. Unlike most kids I knew, I never took my parent for granted. Hell, one had already up and left.

The house was too quiet now, and it was often that I was reminded that I was alone. Since I'd turned eighteen, I was legally allowed to live on my own. A lot of my friends would take having an empty house like it was the perfect opportunity to have nightly ragers. I like to party, but I don't want kids trashing my house. I also don't like the idea of people fucking on my couches or throwing up in bathrooms that I would then have to clean. So, I rarely had people here.

I set my phone down on the bed and sit up, looking at the wall lined with trophies and the jerseys hung above my bed. Each one I've worn since the flag football days. The entire room is covered in sports memorabilia, except for the two large bookcases against the wall opposite my bed.

When I'd seen Harper Posy outside the hunting store with a shirt and some papers, she'd also been holding a copy of *David*

Copperfield. Ever since, I'd been thinking about that damn book in her hand.

Was she at home reading it, in her bed? What was she wearing? Did she like to turn out the lights and use a flashlight, or did she stay up late, the lamp light causing stars to explode in the corners of her eyes.

Walking to my bookcase, I pull out a worn copy of the same book, and flop on my bed. I open it, knowing what the first sentence of the first page will say.

Just like no one sees the real me, no one but my dad and grandpa know that I enjoy reading. When Harper had yelled at me in honors English on Monday, she hadn't realized that I actually did care about the books we were going to read.

What no one knows is that while I am home alone in this house, without parties or girls or even friends, I often read. Dickens, Huxley, Stephen King, J.K. Rowling. I liked it all. I'd even read *Fifty Shades of Grey*. Of course, I had to stop like every other chapter to jack off ... damn, that book was kinky.

Harper pops into my head, and so does the idea of tying her up, Christian Grey style. Shit, now I'm hard. The new girl is an even more innocent virgin than the one in the book.

It would be easy to go to tomorrow's bonfire, the same one the students of Haven throw every Saturday night, and stick my dick in any willing pussy. Get to ten, win bragging rights.

But something about that girl intrigues me. Not in a *I want to hold her hand and confess feelings way*, but I guess I'd just never seen a hot girl actually care about school. At Haven, there are cheerleaders and everyone else. Guess which sect I'd fucked?

And yeah, she was hot. Really hot. When I told her that she had gall to think I'd want to fuck her, I'd just been playing head games with her.

That's how I'd get her. Break down her confidence, call her by the wrong name or some shit. Make her believe she never had a chance with me, and then *wham*. Come on to her so hard that she won't know what hit her. She'd have to sleep with me to prove to herself that a guy like me would want her.

When all along, my scheme will have gone perfectly according to plan.

9

HARPER

A lot of people think boys in high school are sex crazy, riddled with hormones and rabid like horny dogs.

And, they are probably right.

But what they forget is that most girls in high school are obsessed with one thing and one thing only.

Their virginity.

When will they lose it? Who will they give it to? Will it hurt? Has so-and-so already lost it? What will my peers think of me if I give it up too early, or too late?

So many questions, not enough information or maturity to really understand what they're doing. Too many emotions and hormones, driving girls to make stupid decisions.

In Florida, almost every girl I overheard talking about it, who'd decided to give it up, had regretted it. She'd either picked the wrong guy, or hadn't felt the mythical thing you're supposed to feel.

And so I'd decided, freshman year of high school while everyone had been running around, trying as fast as they could to take their clothes off, that I was going to wait. Yes, wait.

I'd never detailed the rules of this waiting, if it was for

marriage or just for a period of time until I thought I was mature enough. But I had made that promise to myself, and I'd kept it. I want my first time to be special, as stupid as that sounds. I want it to mean something, to be with someone I love, to be pleasurable and slow and in control but also out of my head all at the same time.

I mean, I'd never been in the situation to even come close, but it was also because I had never put myself in that position.

Well, I should also add that no boy has ever made me feel the need to get naked, or even close to it. No boy has made my heart thump, or my palms sweat, or my knees shake.

Until Cain Kent.

That boy is like venom to my veins, paralyzing and scorching all at the same time. I lock up around him, my throat constricts and the apex of my thighs becomes slick and uncomfortable. Like I need to rub it desperately. Which is something I've never been curious about, not even a solo exploration.

He's dangerous to my promise. But I know myself, and when it comes down to it, he's the exact opposite of the person I'd break my waiting streak for. So I won't do it.

I'd had my first shift at Hook & Hunt this morning, and all I'd heard over the radio in the shop was how amazing Cain Kent had played in the game the night previous. I wanted to claw my eardrums out, and I'd rolled my eyes too many times to count.

And now I'm sitting in the empty field a few hundred yards from our shabby little ranch house, lying on my back looking at the stars. Saturday nights meant nothing to me, and they really never had. In Florida, the party scene was too riddled with burnouts and reckless sex. It wasn't my thing. I usually spent my weekends working, or at a remote beach writing or plotting in my notebook.

I love my grandmother's property for the fact that it's quiet and secluded.

Except for the last five minutes, I've been hearing random bouts of laughter and the beat of a song floating through the air.

"What the heck is that?" I ask no one in particular.

Getting up, I start to walk toward a patch of trees about half a mile in front of me. And as I get closer, I can make out the flicker of flames between the trunks and leaves.

And then I'm at the tree line, an outsider, a peeping Tom, to a party. Teens, dozens of them, maybe even a hundred, all crowded around a giant bonfire, pickup trucks backed up to it with girls and boys sitting in the beds. One truck is rigged with a giant stereo system in the back, a song by Luke Bryan booming out of the speakers. There are more than a couple of pairs making out, and drunken laughter rings out. Many of the girls are dancing, shaking their long legs and bare shoulders for attention.

They must be on another property, because just knowing my grandmother, she'd never allow trespassers. Especially ones who were participating in underage drinking.

"Do you always sneak up on places you don't belong?"

His voice makes me jump, and dammit how is this guy always an observer to my observing?

"Technically, I'm still on my property. You are the ones partying in the woods where the cops can't find you," I scoff.

Cain chuckles. "Trust me, darling, the cops don't care what we do."

I didn't doubt that. No way would they mark up their perfect athlete's record with an intoxication charge.

It's dark, but it doesn't mean I can't see the outline of his abs and biceps in the gray T-shirt he wears. Simple blue khaki shorts stretch over his thighs, and his hair is messy with its long black strands on the top of his head.

"You weren't at my game last night." His statement surprises, and I have to dig my nails into the palms of my hands to keep from reaching out and touching a muscled arm.

His game. Like he owned the football team and league. And that tone, accusatory. As if how dare I miss his spectacle?

"How would you know that I wasn't there?" I throw back.

"I'm a quarterback, observation is the name of my game. Plus, if you'd seen me play, you would be draped all over me right now. Chicks dig my moves. On the field, and in the bedroom." Cain winks, and while my insides go molten, I hold my position.

My arms are still crossed over my chest, and I scowl. "You're a pig, you know that, right?"

His smile, those straight pearly whites glistening at me, is downright panty-dropping. "I know, but pigs like to get down and dirty. Want to get dirty with me, Harper?"

"I thought it was laughable for you to want to, what did you say? Fuck me?" I take a few steps back, feeling out of place.

"Aw, shucks, sweetheart ... I also told you I know how to tease." He hooks me with that southern twang and I take another involuntary step forward.

He's mesmerizing. A magician of a young girl's emotions ... I don't even like him and yet I'm looking at his lips.

I just convinced myself, mere hours ago, that I had to stay away from him. That he was a threat to my promise to wait.

Yet here I am, inches away from his mouth, alone with him in the woods, those hypnotizing green eyes baiting me.

"I told you to leave me alone." Why I've encountered him so many times in one week can only be billed to fate.

And fate can be one hell of a sarcastic bitch.

"And I think you're a liar."

His hand raises, hovering at the corner of my jaw, not touching me, but just floating there. I can feel the heat from his fingers, smell the alcohol on his breath. It's like he's breathing fire and igniting everything inside of me.

But I fight against the allure. "The only liar standing here is you. Everything about you is a lie."

I'm not sure how I know this, only having met this boy less than a week ago, but I do. Cain Kent is a fraud. He shows one picture to the world and is another work of art entirely.

"An unexciting truth may be eclipsed by a thrilling lie."

His whispered words ring somewhere in my head.

It's not until he's walked off that I realize what, or who, they're from. Cain is holding up a beer and saluting everyone at the party, who in turn cheer back at him. Mr. Haven and his court of subjects.

He quoted Aldous Huxley.

Cain Kent, jock extraordinaire, knows literary passages enough to quote them.

I lift my hand and cup my own jaw where he hadn't even touched me, and marveled.

10

CAIN

The Sons of America Nursing Home sits on old horse ranch land, the large red barn still standing and used as storage for the facility.

"Hi, Nanette." I wave as I walk in, not bothering to sign my name in the visitor's guest log.

They know me. Know I'll be here every Monday, rain or shine.

"Cain! How you doing, sweetheart? Great game on Friday, but you need to ice those ribs, that hit looked brutal!" The middle-aged receptionist with bleach blond hair puffier than sleeves in the 80s made a concerned face.

She wasn't wrong. My ribs were black and blue just three days after Friday night's game, but we got the W so it was all worth it.

"I'll take that to mind, ma'am." I smile.

She blushes. "Now, boy, how many times do I have to tell you? Don't call me ma'am. It makes me feel old."

I shrug and smile again, and walk down the hall. A left at the end, a right past the cafeteria, and then about thirty steps to the fourth door on the right.

"Cain, my boy!" The booming voice echoes out from the doorway as soon as I step in front of it.

He looks tired today. The smell of chemicals and medicine permeate the air in here, like a sterile cologne. The khaki, boring clothing hangs from his slim frame, and I can remember a time when his strong, athletic build inspired me to be a better player.

"Gramps, good to see you." I walk in and shake his hand, the sound of September baseball scratching in and out from the AM radio that was always at his bedside.

Every Monday I visit him, it's our time together and I look forward to it as much as he does. But I knew for him, this was what kept him going. These visits, talking strategy and game play.

"Great game last Friday, but you let those D linemen get the best of you at some points. Don't pay attention to anything else but those two hands holding the ball, and the receiver you're aiming at. Fuck those bullies trying to intimidate you across the line. Don't let 'em spook you."

He wastes no time getting down to brass tacks, and I know he's been foaming at the mouth to give me his Monday morning, or afternoon in this case, quarterback speech. No pun intended.

I always take his advice as gospel, because he's been there. Gramps knows what he's talking about. "Says the former defensive lineman. You calling yourself a bully."

He winks. "The best bully of 'em all."

My grandfather played in the biggest league of them all, the one that every young football player strives to make it to. But a diagnosis of Parkinson's ended his career at thirty, and had him in a nursing home by the time he was sixty. Now, he's confined to a wheelchair, barely has the use of his hands, and the left side of his body constantly shakes while the right side is almost rigid and statue-like.

While he still has the ability to talk and chew, his quality of life is declining. I try to put on a brave face for him, try not to stare at his jerky body movements. I hold my breath when his aides have to get him in bed or onto the toilet, and I always feed him when he asks. This disease is a horrible one, but I hope that I make Gramps' days just a little better. He's part of the reason I play so hard, want to win so badly. So that he can get some joy from it.

We talk football for a little while longer, and then he asks about school. Gramps gets it, he was in my shoes. Football is life, and everything else comes second.

But he also knows what it's like to be in love. He married my grandmother when he was twenty and was with her up until she passed ten years ago. And he also knows that you have to have a backup plan if this career path fails. Luckily, he'd played enough years on his inflated contract to save and not have to worry about money.

Gramps could've gone to any of the top facilities in Texas, but he chose to stay at this decent one in Haven because it's his hometown too, and it's closer to me.

"I bet you have all of those girls in a tizzy." He laughs, wheezing at the end of his fit.

"I learned from the best." I pat his hand.

"You didn't learn that from me. I loved Adeline from the time I was fifteen until the day she died. There is something to be said about a fun time, but there is something so much more fulfilling in loving a good woman. And your grandmother, she was a good woman."

He starts to get teary and I have to look away. I'll never understand that kind of love, because I've never had it. While I have a good dad and a good grandfather, the love of a woman is something I missed. My grandmother was always too preoccupied with Gramps and his Parkinson's, and my mother left before I even knew her.

I'd never understand what the big deal was when it came to falling in love with a girl.

"Oh, come on, Cain. Isn't there any pretty gal at school that peaks your interest?" He smiles like the naïve Gramps that he is.

Why oh why, when he says that, does the damn fawn of a girl come into my head?

I'd quoted Huxley to her, like some kind of romantic nerd. That wasn't what I was trying to do. I was trying to have sex with her, though neither she nor anyone else knew that.

How had I decided so quickly that I wanted in Harper Posy's pants? And why, after she'd spoken to me like I was a gross pervert, was I still trying to strategize my plan of attack?

It made me curl my fist, because I wasn't keeping score but if I was, she had a leg up on me. And being down is something I never settle for.

I let it simmer in my veins, put it on the back burner for the rest of my visit with Gramps.

But it was still there lurking, and I knew that sooner or later, I was going to come out on top.

11

HARPER

"I have a date."

Mom claps her hands excitedly as she sits on her bed, all of her makeup laid out in front of her.

I was wondering how long it would take. Apparently, two weeks is the answer.

After another week of school, which passed by uneventfully to my delight; we've settled into Haven pretty well. I've been excelling in my classes, and it was refreshing to have honors courses where the students actually competed against one another. Healthy competition made me work harder, and because my brain was firing on all cylinders, I was like a writing machine.

I'd finished another three chapters of two thousand words each in my book. A young adult suspense novel, it was coming together piece by piece. I'd plotted, mapped out chapters, and begun work on it almost a year and a half ago. I thought I was writing too slowly, but I tried to be kind to my mind and creativity because I wanted to produce the best book possible for my debut.

Mom found a job at one of the local elementary schools, a

position filling in for another teacher out on maternity leave. It wasn't permanent, but it paid, and there was hope for future employment.

She and Grandma had been getting along. Or well ... coexisting, I should say. They pretty much ignored each other, but it hadn't led to any blowups, so I was happy about that.

"Who is it with?" I ask reluctantly, because I'm too used to this.

She smiles a mega-watt grin and slicks mascara over her lashes. "This gorgeous guy I went to high school with. We never dated, but I always thought he was *so* cute. And then I bumped into him at the coffee shop two days ago, and he asked me out. Can you believe it?"

Of course I could, my mother was gorgeous. And vivacious. While I thought I was pretty myself, I looked almost nothing like her. Where I was fair and blond and almost a plain kind of pretty, my mother was dark features and tumbling hair and a waistline that most would kill for. I inherited a lot of my looks from my father. Except for the oversized breasts and blue eyes, those I got from Mom.

"That's ... great." Even I hear the lack of enthusiasm in my voice.

"You think it's a bad idea." My mother's mood is spoiled like a child on Halloween who didn't get their favorite candy.

I sit on her bed, the same one she slept in when she was a teenager. "I just ... remember why we had to move here? Do you think it's the best idea to date someone from Haven. Especially given that you're from Haven?"

We hadn't talked much about how weird it was for her to back in her hometown. But I could only imagine.

From the way Mom tells stories, Haven is where her glory days took place. Even though she had strict, farmer parents, she was the ultimate, popular Southern belle. She won homecoming and prom queen multiple years in a row. Was captain of the cheer squad. Thinking about that made me shudder thinking of Annabelle Mills. Anyway, this was where Mom spent years with friends and crushes, drank in the woods and tubed down the lake.

She'd talk to me as a child about her hometown like it was some kind of euphoric suburbia, and now that I was here, I had yet to think about how strange it must be for her to be back.

Mom picks my hand up off the bed. "Harper ... this makes me feel good. Going on dates. You may think I'm ditzy or just some silly romantic. But ... for me to keep believing that love is out there? I need to date. I need to get dressed up and have the attention of a man on me. For someone to tell me I'm pretty and look at me with that look, even if it's just for one night. I need to keep hoping that it's out there, that I didn't lose the only love that will ever be sent my way."

I know she's talking about my father, even though she doesn't say it. She rarely talks about him, I know it hurts her too much.

Clearing my throat so as not to give away the emotion in my voice, I nod. "Okay, then. I hope your date is fantastic."

She smiles and pats my knee before I rise. I stop in the kitchen and grab my laptop, and head for the back porch to write for the night. No sitting in the fields for me on weekend nights anymore. I knew I would be able to hear the sounds of my peers, and that meant Cain was somewhere out there. He and the woods were haunting my dreams enough.

Sometime a little later, I hear tires crunch up the gravel drive, and my mom calls out goodbye before the sound of the screen door slamming echoes through the house.

I don't want to see boyfriend number whatever, because most likely, he's a jerk. But I'll support my mom however she wants.

My fingers clack away at the keyboard, my main character just having found a mysterious key in her basement, along with a map to a secret buried somewhere in the forest in town. I'm so wrapped up in the story that I don't hear my grandmother come out.

"I brought you some sweet tea, you looked like you could use a little." She sits in the rocker next to mine.

Looking up, I see two frosty glasses of brown liquid on the table between us. "Thank you."

She nods, looking off into the distance, over every piece of her land. "Haven, Texas has the most beautiful sunsets around. Can't beat 'em. You should put that in your book there."

It's the first time she's tried to make conversation with me about anything other than chores or work.

"How did you know I was writing a book?"

Her eyes crinkle, and her gray strands blow in the wind. "I may not know much about computers, but I do know how to look over people's shoulders. Especially little girls who are, how do they say it? Screen-locked?"

My mouth falls open. "You have been spying on me? Wow, Grandma. I don't know what to say."

"You could tell me a little about it." She finally looks at me, the same eyes that my mother and I have staring back into my own.

I kick off, rocking a bit as the sun slips behind one of the rolling hills. I can make out the outline of horses in the distance. "You really want to know about my writing?"

Something in her eyes looks sad. "Now, don't go telling your mother this, ya hear?"

I nod, not sure where this is going. It seems to placate her and she goes on.

"When she was young ... I wasn't the most supportive of mothers. I didn't know anything about having dreams, I grew up in a family you weren't allowed to have them in. Maybe if I had listened to her more, she wouldn't have run off right after graduation. Maybe I would have been in her life. In your life. These are the things you look back on when you're a crotchety old woman like me. So yes, I'd like to hear about your book."

Two times in one night, the only two women I know as family have opened up to reveal something deeply personal to me. I'm not sure what's happening. Maybe it's the pink and purple sunset descending on the old ranch.

So I tell her. I explain the plot, the genre, how I found out about publishing my own novel without having to go the traditional route. How I was going to meticulously edit it myself, because I didn't have the money to hire someone. How I'd taught myself Photoshop and had already made a simple, but eye-catching cover. Again, because I couldn't afford to pay someone else to do it. I tell my grandmother about the community I'd found and how social media could help immensely when you had no marketing budget.

By the end, she was staring at me like I had just told her aliens existed. "And you did all of this ... on your own?"

I shrug, embarrassed by her astonishment. "I didn't really have a lot of friends in Florida. And well, I've loved books my entire life."

Grandma takes a sip of her sweet tea and turns out to the sky again, which is now almost dark. "I like a woman with drive. You and only you can take care of yourself. If you never forget that, you'll always succeed."

I think I am going to have to put that kernel of wisdom in my book.

12

CAIN

Somewhere, I'm bleeding.

It's under my uniform, so I can't see it, but I know that it's there. Not that I pay it much attention, because we're down by three going into the last two minutes of this game and I'm so laser-focused that it feels like the one time Grady dared us all to do Adderall.

The scent of mud and grass fills my nose, the lights of Haven High School's football stadium beat down on my padded jersey. It's a home game, which means that the bleachers are packed with screaming fans, some of them without shirts on, chests painted in the late September chill. Our team stands on the sidelines, second-stringers and defensive players all nervously pacing back and forth, chewing on their mouth guards.

Despite the dropping temperatures, I'm burning up. Sweat drips from my temples, and I'm clenching my jaw as coach screams at me to get this play done and score. Fourth quarter comebacks always make him jumpy, but I know that I've got this. This is what I live for, my lifeblood.

I talk to my guys in our huddle like a general going into war.

Each of their faces is pinched and focused, eyes dilated, black paint smeared down their cheeks. Long gone is the fun of half-time, where we peaked out the locker room door to check out the homecoming court girls in their sexy little dresses parading out on the field.

We break, taking no time at all to get into our positions. I call the play, see the defense shift, and call an audible. Immediately my guys move, my receivers switch, I tick off different words to let them know what we're going with off the cuff.

And then I call it, and everything moves. The ground vibrates, growls burst forth. But for me, for my quarterback brain, it all moves in slow motion. Like I'm that superhero in the *Justice League* movie who can run really fast ... can't think of his name just now.

I hand the ball off to our running back, Trey, and he does a spin move around one of their lineman, gaining twelve yards and a first down.

We're thirty yards from the end zone, and while I could move it slow and steady, I don't want to. I want fireworks.

Yeah, I'm in the mood for glory tonight.

It's homecoming, let's give them something to talk about.

On the next play, I don't even huddle. I call out our Hail Mary formation, and some of the guys glance at me but do as their told. There is still a minute on the clock, we don't need to score yet. But I want to, and I know this our best shot.

The clicking in my brain says so.

I give the command.

They move.

Click. Click. Click.

Without even narrowing my gaze on Emmitt, I launch the ball, sending it soaring in an arc so perfect, it could touch the moon if that's where I'd wanted it to go.

But it doesn't.

Instead, it lands in my receiver's outstretched arms.

Which are in the end zone.

I'm tackled, but it's by my teammates, not the guys who desire to chop my body in half at this moment. The crowd is going insane in the stands. I can hear them shouting my battle cry, the chant they repeat every time I throw a touchdown.

Raise the Cain!

Raise the Cain!

Yeah, it's going to be a hell of a homecoming weekend.

"Fuck, I wish they would turn this shit off. Play some Aldean!"

Emmitt is yelling at the DJ, and he's so hammered that he's already sweated through his shirt and tie.

The dance floor, which is really just the tile of our cafeteria with all of the lunch tables cleared out, pulses with energy. Every which way you look, guys grind up on girls, with girls pushing their asses back on the guys crotches. Guaranteed that every person with a dick in this room is semi-hard, and now I'm weirded out looking at all of these guys who are probably sporting boners.

Right now, a nameless blonde who looks like most girls here, short dress and curled hair, gyrates on my cock, and I hold her hips, maneuvering them.

The alcohol has all but worn off in the half hour we've been here, and I curse myself because I should have snuck in a flask like Emmitt.

And since my buzz is wearing off, and the tie around my neck is fucking strangling me, I'm not feeling this girl at all. Walking away without an explanation, I stalk off the dance floor. Someone around here has to have booze. I don't know why I let the guys convince me to come to the actual dance for homecoming, the afterparty was always better and I could actually have my dick played with outside of my pants.

At the tables on the side, some people are sitting solo. Some drink water, hydrating before going back out there. And others are making out, hands in places that the teachers or chaperones definitely didn't approve of.

Toward the back, two girls catch my eye.

One of them being Harper Posy.

Shock courses through me, because for some reason I didn't think this would be her scene at all. No, I *know* this isn't her scene. She hasn't been at any of our football games since she moved to town, and I was sour to admit that I knew she hadn't been in the crowd. I'd looked.

Harper also never came to bonfires or parties, and the time I'd caught her lurking was a fluke. Since the night in the woods, I haven't seen her on the back acres of her grandmother's property. I should have put two and two together when she moved in there, since the land that Grady's parents own borders the ranch land.

My mind drifts back to that bonfire as I look at her in the back corner of the cafeteria. Her surprised gasp when I'd snuck up on her, the way she smelled like summer leaves and the fireflies twinkled around her pale hair. I'd been so close, so close to taking those plump cherry lips.

I shake my head. After our win last night, we were untouchable. Gods. If I wanted to have a threesome tonight, I could probably convince just about any girl here to get naked with me.

But there she is, standing in the corner while Mary-Kate tries to drag her out of her chair. Her hair hangs long down her back, like it usually does, and she's wearing a plain black dress that hugs those massive tits. It doesn't fit right, which makes her cleavage pop out even more. I was sporting a midi by the time I made it to her.

"Come on, Harper. One dance? You know you want to shimmy." I overhear Mary-Kate slur at the new girl.

She, like most everyone here, had a couple of pre-dance drinks. Probably in the backseat of someone's truck in the parking lot before chewing a piece of gum on the way in to showing one of the teacher's at the entrance their tickets.

"Yeah, new girl, why don't you dance?" I send a vicious smile her way.

Both Harper and Mary-Kate look up at me, and the latter is stunned.

"Cain?" Mary-Kate sputters.

Not because she is infatuated with me, like most of the girls here, but because she has no idea that I know Harper, outside of the time she yelled at me in English. No one does really. As of now, we've had our dalliances in the shadows. Secrets whispered and tension unspoken.

"MK." I tip my head. And then move to Harper, my eyes falling down her body. Shit, there was nothing sexier than an untouched chick. "How about it? Just once dance."

"I think you should dance with him." Mary-Kate smiles and pushes her friend toward me.

Finally, Harper looks up at me. "No, thanks. I don't dance."

"Good thing I'm a great one, then. Dancer, that is. I'll lead." I offer my hand, total gentleman-like.

I think she can tell I'm not going away, and if this will get us both off of her back so she can go home then she'll do it. Because her expression relents. "Fine, whatever."

Her hand slaps into mine, like she's annoyed she has to do this in the first place. It's small and warm, her fingers slender and non-committal to the show of affection. The exact opposite of what a good handshake should be, her digits are like limp fish sticks.

But I keep it moving, ignoring the pull in my chest while my large fingers stroke at her skin as I walk us to the dance floor.

And of course, the second we move onto the makeshift dance floor, all ready to connect our bodies nice and close together and turn her body into a pile of mush that I could mold, is when the beat turns slow and Brad Paisley begins crooning about love.

Shit.

I don't stop though, because I asked for this dance and I can still play her body like an instrument I know like the back of my hand. I've been told I'm an expert when it comes to girl's bodies, and Harper definitely won't be hard to break.

Even if she's proven to be a worthy opponent thus far.

"You look mighty sexy tonight." I smirk as I leer at her tits.

"Gosh, you just make a girl feel special." She rolls her eyes.

My hands circle her waist, pulling her into me so that she has no choice but to wrap her arms around my neck. She's slim and shorter than me, and she feels ... dainty in my arms. We sway to the music, and Harper avoids eye contact as much as possible.

"This doesn't seem like your scene." I bend down so that she has to look into my eyes.

Harper shrugs, licks her lips. "I've never been to a school dance before. Figured this was my last shot. Plus, Mary-Kate wouldn't leave it alone."

"You've never been to a school dance? Where have you been living, under a rock?"

Harper scowls at me. "Where I'm from in the Florida Keys, kids are more interested in dime bags and blow than prom and senior skip day."

I'd never asked where she'd moved from. In fact, I'd never asked much of anything about her.

I'm about to ask her about where she's from and why she moved, what she likes ... when my cock gets the better of me. It's nestled right up against her stomach, she must feel it, and it's only repeating one thing.

The tenth girl. The tenth girl.

Why do I care where she's from or if she likes to watch movies or TV shows? This is about getting in her pants, not into her head. Who the hell am I right now? Slow dances and conversation.

Without permission, without tenderness, I bend down and harshly take her lips.

It's not in private, as if I'm saying to her that having any type of special moment with her is off the table. That she's not significant, that she's just like every other girl here getting tongued and finger fucked under their dresses.

My lips are bruising, crushing, and I can tell that she's inexperienced. Somewhere in my chest, a flicker of guilt nips at me. Harper can't keep up with me, her lips and tongue fumbling. The naivety actually kind of turns me on, and I skate my hands up her ribcage and back down, around to cup and grip her ass.

Everything in me is lighting up like a wall of elevator buttons, and I can tell that she's into it because she's mewling into my mouth.

My hands at her ass, I start to pry at the fabric, raising it higher. Our lips dance just like we do, and something more than fucking with our mouths is happening.

This feeling, hot and then cold and then hot, is new. The goose bumps, the semi-nauseous feeling low in my gut. The fear.

What the fuck?

Even though it's a slow song, that doesn't stop one of my

football buddies from passing on the dance floor and saying too loudly, "Get it, Kent!"

Automatically, Harper stops. She's still in my arms, the music still floats over our heads, and others around us are none the wiser to the football star and the new girl just having made out.

But her eyes, those piercing baby blues, are shaken. I know I've became a splinter under her skin, she's not going to be able to shake me now. Harper Posy will fall asleep every night from here to eternity thinking about the kiss I just planted on her inexperienced lips.

And then she does something so unexpected, I bristle.

She laughs. A tinkling, melodic sound that grates my nerves but tightens my nuts.

"You might have won the battle, but you're definitely going to lose the war." Harper smirks, a sneaky expression that has my hackles rising.

"And why is that?" I'm so confused. There is nothing simple about this girl.

Was I still sure I wanted to make her number ten?

"Because I'm never going to sleep with you, Cain Kent." She sees right through me.

I play with a piece of her white-blond hair. Her shiver tells me that her body thinks otherwise. "I told you I didn't want to fuck you."

"We both know that's all you *do* want to do with me. And I'm here to tell you that it's never going to happen. Because ... I'm never going to sleep with anyone. Not until I'm in love, that is."

Her confession stuns me, and I'm rendered speechless for a full minute. And during that minute, Harper decides it's her time to escape. She walks off without a backward glance.

"Dude, were you just kissing the new girl? The one who schooled you in English?" Grady walks up, his tie askew and pants unbuttoned. He definitely just got laid in the bathroom.

"I told you, that one is mine. She's going to be my number ten."

I was going for bonus points at the end of this competition, and Harper had just unknowingly thrown down the best gauntlet of them all.

Virgin pussy.

13

HARPER

I'm staring at Mary-Kate's ceiling, the fan whirling above my head.

Just like the last five nights of this long week, I can't fall asleep. Or close my eyes. Or dream.

Because every time I do, I see Cain Kent's face. His mouth, coming down on mine, the roughness of his kiss. The growl he'd emitted when I'd reciprocated.

I'd been kissed, but never like that. *Nothing* quite like that.

It haunted me in my waking and sleeping moments. Why had I allowed Cain to get to me? He knew, he *had* to know, that I was staring at the ceiling, thinking about that kiss. I blush all the way down to my toes, which are currently under Mary-Kate's comforter, thinking of how bad of a kisser I must have been. Cain Kent must have kissed dozens, maybe even hundreds, of girls ... all of whom were probably much more skilled than I was.

I had no idea what I was doing. I let him sweep me along, trying to mimic his movements even as my brain short-circuited from what his mouth was doing. But it hadn't stopped my body from warming to Cain. I'd woken up every night this week in a sweaty panic, my underwear soaked from the arousal my dreams brought on.

What is wrong with me? I'd sworn to myself that I'd keep my distance from Cain. I didn't even know the guy, and I'd agreed to slow dance with him and had then allowed him to maul me in the most public place possible. I wasn't stupid enough not to know that I was just another girl on his list.

Gah, I had to stop thinking about him and that kiss.

"Did you just growl?" MK turns over, the room dark except for her night-light shaped like the Eiffel Tower.

MK had insisted I sleepover tonight, Friday night, since the football team had a bye week and I'd accidentally revealed that I'd never had the ritual sleepover. So, she'd invited Imogen over, and together, we'd pigged out on popcorn, chocolate, painted each other's toenails, and yes, had even braided hair.

Imogen had gone home around eleven, and I'd yawned and brushed my teeth much to MK and her late night plan's dismay.

I hadn't realized I'd done it out loud. "Ugh, yes."

"Spill. Sleepovers are all about gossip and pillow talk. But what is said at the sleepover, stays at the sleepover." MK pretends to zip her lips and throw away the key.

She was quickly becoming a good friend, and a confidant, and I needed someone to talk to. I was going to burst.

"You know that I kissed Cain, right?" I sigh.

MK chuckles. "I don't think anyone at homecoming missed that little public display of affection. You've been the envy of half the school, if you didn't realize."

Maybe that was why half the girls at school said hi to me now, and half looked like they wanted to murder me. "God, I'm such a statistic. Just the next girl in the lineup of Cain Kent."

"It was really that bad? If you dislike him so much, then who cares? It was only a kiss."

"To me, kissing is a big deal." I shove my hand under my head, looking at her on the other pillow.

MK props up on her elbow. "Wait a second, are you a virgin?"

"Yes," I grumble, but then I stiffen my upper lip. "By choice. I want to wait until ... I know it sounds stupid and cliché, but until I'm in love."

She flops back down and looks at me. "That's not stupid, Harper. Not stupid in the least. I think a lot of girls wish they'd waited, me included. I lost my V-card in the back of a pickup after a night of drinking with a boy who doesn't even bother to return my calls. Ain't that a freaking cliché?"

I can practically feel her eye roll across the queen sized bed. "I'm sorry, MK. And I don't mean to sound insensitive, but that's exactly what I don't want. I don't need candles and flowers, but love and comfort and trust are big factors in my decision to have sex. And Cain Kent is guaranteed to supply none of those. So I'm annoyed that I'm now linked to him because of one stupid moment of weakness."

She studies me. "You can't stop thinking about it, can you? And not because you regret it, but because you want to do it again."

I hit her with the edge of my pillow. "What are you, psychic?"

"No, I just speak the same language. We're teenage girls, Harper. We crave the bad boy, we want for the things we know we shouldn't touch. It's imprinted in our DNA at this age."

"I can promise you, I've never wanted the bad boy before. Something about Cain, it just gets under my skin."

MK is silent a moment, and then looks at me. "I'm not saying this because we're girls and we try to psych each other up about boys. But ... he's different. I can't put my finger on it, but there is something that happens when he sees you, and I've known the boy since kindergarten. Hell, everyone in Haven has known everyone else since diapers. You're not exactly his type, either."

I prop up on an elbow now, too curious to appear nonchalant. "Oh? And what is his type?"

She shrugs, the sounds of a coyote somewhere outside howling. "He likes the easy, hot girls. The ones who are good for a roll in the hay, and then a see you later with a pat on the ass. Cain doesn't work for much, and he gets almost anything he wants."

"Almost anything?"

"I keep forgetting you're new. I guess it's because I like you so much and we're friends." She squeezes my hand across the mattress. "But, Cain's mom left their family when he was young. Maybe elementary school, but I can't remember. Just up and left, and from what everyone in town knows, hasn't been heard of since. Anyway, he's always been broken up about it, as one would be. Hasn't been the same since, and his relationship with women ... it's tricky. His dad is in the military, deploys so much that he's never home. Rumor is, he can't go back to the house that his wife left. So, Cain is pretty much alone. There is some heavy emotional stuff there, and even though he acts like a badass, I think that deep down there is just a hurt little boy in there. After all, no man uses his penis like that if he doesn't have some issues going on in his head and heart."

Her insight leaves me speechless, and gives me a whole other side to Cain that blossoms, revealing itself so that my mind digests just how much he has been through.

Here I was, thinking that the school's notorious jock was just that, and that he got everything he wished for.

Turns out, we are more alike than I'd ever even thought. A parent gone. A parent protecting the world in spite of how dangerous it is, and how you may never come back to your family.

MK yawns and turns over, mumbling something about

having a good talk, and then I hear her breathing even out and I know that she's asleep.

I don't want this new information that I've learned about Cain to soften my stance on him, but it does.

I feel my resolve beginning to crack like a huge iceberg splitting in two. And I know I have to triage to keep the damage from getting any worse.

14

CAIN

"Dude, do you think the number of girls we fuck talk to each other?" Grady asks.

I've thought about this before, and I know we've had drunken talks about it among the six of us competing to get to ten.

"Nah, or else no one would still sleep with us," Joshua, pipes up.

It's Sunday, our day of rest, or in this case, drinking on the river. The river is more of a creek, with shallow beds of rocks and muddy banks of grass along its path. But, it was what we had here in Haven, and on a Sunday, seniors and townies alike could be found throwing one back while listening to the latest country playlist on Spotify.

"That's true, although ... I feel like girls would still fuck us even if they knew." Emmitt shrugs, swigging beer from his bottle of Bud Light.

"I added another one this weekend." Paul smirks, cradling his lax stick like only a lax bro does.

Paul and Joshua are football players with us, but also go out for lacrosse in the spring. They're not superstars in either, which is why they play more than one sport. They'll probably end up at division three schools, where they'll be happy to half-dedicate themselves to sports and fully dedicate themselves to partying.

"I call bullshit, you were only at five!" Grady, always the showboat, pops a can of PBR with his keys and shot guns it, even though no one is racing him.

"Nope, I saw the beginnings of it. Cassidy Gollic, he got her good." Joshua fist bumps his teammate, his chocolate skin not frying under the sunlight like the rest of ours is.

"That hot sophomore with the belly button ring? Damn, she's smokin'." Emmitt high fives Paul too.

"How about our resident front runner? Did you get number ten yet?" Grady eyes me.

I've been lounging back on the blanket laid on a patch of damp grass, slowly making my way through my first beer, and now these assholes want to compare dick size. I know who will win, but they're making me pull up the brim of my baseball hat and toss it in the ring. I'm annoyed.

"When I fuck her, you'll know. And you'll also owe me the keys to The Atrium." I grin.

"'Ol buddy here picked the new girl as his last conquest. I figure you're just giving us time to catch up, putting a handicap on yourself. She's never going to take her panties off for you," Grady taunts.

Paul gapes at me. "That hot new girl who kind of looks like Daenerys from *Game of Thrones*? Dude, I know your abilities, but I'm telling you, one look at her and I know she won't give it up. That girl is not the type of girl who is going to cave."

"You saying she's a virgin?" Emmitt wonders. He's trying not to scratch at the brand new tattoo he got done on his ribs, and instead is pulling at his close-cropped brown hair like a mental patient.

I shrug, and the guys talk amongst themselves, discussing

whether or not Harper has had her cherry popped. I know for a fact that she hasn't, because she all but told me. But I don't need to tell these hound dogs that. They'll be salivating after her like a piece of steak in a lion's den.

"I think we should throw a party at The Atrium. It's been too long, and we need to be reminded what we're playing for." Joshua suggests this.

"I couldn't agree more." I smile a devilish expression. "Crazy shit happens at those parties."

Last time we threw a party at the notorious spot, I'd done my first tablet of ecstasy and felt up two girls for more than two hours. The feeling of their skin on my hands was enough to make me shoot my load. Shit is dangerous, it makes the entire world feel like a vibrator or something.

But there won't be any more drugs for me. That was nearly a year ago, when I hadn't yet had college offers on the table and could still get away with stupid shit. Now, I was committed to the best college in the state, and pretty much the country, and had everything riding on it.

Beer and pussy, that was what I could stick to now. Which was fine, drugs had never really been my thing.

"Next Saturday night?" Grady suggests. "We're going to wipe the floor with those pussies from East Jude."

Our Friday night game was a layup, and then we'd be undefeated heading into our last three games of the regular season. Then two weeks of playoffs, and hopefully state. Another state championship in my belt would be a hell of a bargaining chip when it came to college. It would show them that I knew how to run plays, control an offense, and hopefully not be treated like the fresh meat coming in.

"Sounds perfect to me. Emmitt, you get it rolling. You're always the best at that." I give my friend a thumbs-up.

"On it, boss." He starts furiously typing on his phone.

An hour later, I'm lying on my couch, detoxing from the weekend and finishing the last of my homework that's due for the week. Despite what many think, I'm actually a pretty good student. English and math come naturally to me, which is why I'm in honors courses. And science and history aren't far behind, although I chose to stay in the normal courses for those classes just to give myself less homework and more time for football. I technically wasn't going to college for academics, but it felt good to know that I had them to fall back on.

I just downplayed this fact around school, deciding to own my jock status because it was easier than having people fawn over the fact that I was smart and good at sports. That may sound cocky or dickish, but it was true.

My phone buzzes on the coffee table next to the brown leather sectional that takes up most of our living room, and I turn it over to see who is calling.

Coach McDaniels, the man who would mold and shape me for four years to come, was on the other end.

"Hi, Coach." I try to sound more manly than I actually am.

"Kent, how you doing?" His voice is gruff, and to the point.

He calls me every couple of weeks, just to check in. Since it is after September first of my senior year, he was allowed to do that according to NCAA rules. And both he and his alma matter in Austin want to make sure that I am fully committed, that I wasn't going to back out. They want me as much as I want them, which feels good ... but is also another enormous weight added to the pile on my shoulders.

"Good, Coach, feeling really good. Practicing hard, keeping my grades up." What does he expect me to say? I'm terrified of this man, and I'd never want to do anything to disappoint him.

He is the guy who was going to make or break me when it came to the paramount level of football that I wanted to achieve.

"That's good to hear. I watched your game film from last

week, you played well. Just need to keep those feet planted, and I'd like to see some more short passing as opposed to long bombs."

I make a mental note to work on both of those things. "Absolutely, Coach, I can try to improve those things."

"Good, son. All right, well, good luck in the game on Friday, and I'll check in soon."

He hung up without waiting for my goodbye, which he could do because he was the winningest coach in college football.

And I was going to be his quarterback come next August. I'm not a religious man, but right then, I shot up a silent prayer that everything continued on the path that it was on. My brain, and its ability to read defense. My body, and my arm … that I didn't get injured.

And my focus and dedication, because Jesus knows that was the only thing that differentiated amateurs from pros.

15

CAIN

Todd stands at the front of the class, with the words Great Expectations written on the white board behind his head.

"Pip is tough on himself when he doesn't pick the morally right way, and that guilt propels him to try harder in the future. Self-improvement is *the* central theme that Dickens' conveys in this book. Whether it's status, education, or even morals, the novel really plays to the theme of bettering one's self. Why do you think he wanted to drive that point home?"

Harper begins to talk, because Todd doesn't believe in raising hands. "Because self-improvement is really the point of life. Everyone is trying to become the next best version of themselves. Whether it's superficial like beauty or fitness. Whether they want to fall in love because they're single, or be married because they're in love. To learn more, or become more. A medical student wants to be a doctor, everyone always wants a promotion."

Todd nods, and peers around for someone to jump onto that thought.

Lauren, a girl near the windows, speaks up. "I agree to a certain extent. But I think that one of the other themes of the novel, that Pip learns toward the end, is that self-improvement also comes at a cost. Maybe, if he'd just stayed in a certain spot in life, he would have been happier than if he'd tried to climb that ladder."

I can't stop the words from tumbling out of my mouth. "That's definitely true for Estella. She would have probably been better off if she'd just stayed poor, as the daughter of Magwich. Because she was upper crust, it stole her ability to love or sympathize. And although she didn't want to hurt Pip, she warned him she always would, she did it anyway. She was incapable of happiness."

The entire class has turned around to look at me, but the only eyes I see are the color of the ocean and seeing into my forehead.

Harper says quietly, "Suffering has been stronger than all other teaching, and has taught me to understand what your heart used to be. I have been bent and broken, but, I hope, into a better shape."

She quotes the book just as I have, and no one seems to think this is weird, because the discussion continues to Todd's delight. But for the entire rest of the class, neither of us says anything. We also don't break the eye contact that started the moment she spoke her last quote. For fifteen full minutes, we stare at each other, searching the other's face, making expressions, trying to talk without words.

It's the most intimate I've ever been with another human being, and we're not even touching. We're not even speaking.

It's as if Harper knows I've suffered ... maybe she's been asking around?

A part of me feels naked, vulnerable, and it's freaking me out but I also know that she feels the exact same way. And if she feels the same way, that means she's letting me in. That means that I could possibly get inside of her in other ways.

My brain twists on me, moving over to the sick part that doesn't trust women and only thinks with the brain inside of my dick. I convince myself that this is the right way to be, that fucking her and never calling her again will be a good solution since we won't even be in the same town for much longer. College makes everything finite.

If she thinks that my suffering has bent me into a better person, that she can see the good in my heart or some other bullshit like that, she's got another thing coming.

The bell rings and our trance is over; the other students around us getting up and filing out. Harper suddenly gets up and bolts, and I get up, gather my stuff in my arms, and go after her. No backpack for me, I'm one of those idiot jocks who thinks it's cool to be seen with nothing attached. Which usually means that I'm carrying around piles of books since I actually do care about my classes. The no-backpack thing seems so fucking stupid right now.

"Peep, wait up." I trot after her, people in the hallway turning to look at us as I catch up to her.

She slows, and I'm surprised. "Hey."

Harper's voice sounds almost ... kind.

"So, you like Dickens?" I shove my hands in my short pockets.

"I like most any author. What I'm surprised about is that you like Dickens." She eyes me, those blue pools questioning my motives.

She should be ... questioning my motives, that is. "There are a lot of things you don't know about me."

Almost to herself, Harper says, "I'm beginning to think that's true."

"So, that means you'll come hang out with me?" I raise an eyebrow, inflecting a flirty charm into my voice.

It doesn't seem to work on this girl. "Tell me ... is *Great Expectations* your favorite Dickens' novel?"

I shrug and lie through my teeth. "It was an okay read for class. I have to keep my grades up to play football, only reason I keep doing homework."

Harper stops next to a locker, number two hundred and thirty, and smirks. "No one who can quote passages of a book like that has only read said book once. You've analyzed the text, the meaning has sunk into your bones, as it does when you read a truly good piece of literature. You don't fool me, Cain."

She's got my ticket and punched it. Jesus, this girl is so unfazed, and this is even after I stuck my tongue in her mouth at homecoming.

Leaning in as she twirls the combination on her locker, I rub a long lock of hair between two fingers. "Good, so I don't have to bullshit you when I say that I find you hot."

I hear her intake of breath, see the blush creep up her creamy pale neck. Harper stays quiet.

"Because I do. And I've been thinking about how you kissed me—"

"You kissed me." She turns her head, her hair still tangled in my fingers.

It's silky and I wonder what it will look like spread out while she's beneath me. "It wasn't exactly one-sided."

Harper tips her head as if to say touché.

I press on. "So, I think that you should come to this party I'm throwing."

"I think that your parties are something a little over my excitement level." Those cherry-colored lips look edible, and I can't help staring while she talks.

"I promise I'll take it at your speed." Letting her think we're playing her game will help me get the victory I desire.

She hikes an eyebrow up. "Yeah, I really believe that."

I let go of her hair and hold up three fingers. "Scouts honor."

Harper hoots out a laugh. "Oh God, you're so far from a Boy Scout, it's insane."

"Bad Boy Scout, at your service." I salute, and I see the joke dance in her eyes as she digests it.

I'm weakening her resolve.

"That sounds about right. Instead of building fires and hiking trails, you're badges are in beer funneling and hook ups." Harper shuts her locker and begins to move down the hallway, not waiting for me.

"So that means you'll come to my party? You can't go wrong with a guy who is known for those skills."

She looks at me as we walk, and then stops. The bell rings, and I can see that she wants to hurry to her next class. "If I see the guy that just quoted Dickens to me, then ... yeah, I'll go."

I've caught my canary. "Good, I'll pick you up, give me your phone."

Picking a girl up showed that you were a gentleman. It showed that you were committed to spending time with her during the night. Showing Harper how nice I could be would only serve to soften her more, thus making her more willing to get naked with me.

"Why would I give you my phone? Plus, we're in school, I don't have it."

I roll my eyes. "I'm not a teacher, don't lie about not having your phone. I want to put my number in and text myself so that I can give you the party details."

She scans the hallway, and then pulls a cell phone about three generations old from her back pocket. I quickly type my number in and text myself.

"Now you can sext me whenever you like." I grin at her.

Harper scoffs and hits my bicep. "I have to go to class."

She's flirting. That's a good sign. "I'll see you this weekend."

16

HARPER

Cain starts texting me on Saturday afternoon, and my stomach is in knots the entire conversation.

Cain: *Hey*

Harper: *Hey*

Cain: *Still coming to my party tonight?*

Harper: *Depends ... who is coming to pick me up? Cain the football player or Cain the Dickens' fan?*

Cain: *Actually, this week it's Dan Brown. Am I still going to get a good night kiss?*

He was flirting with me. Text flirting. I'd heard about this, had attempted to do it with one guy back in Florida, but had failed miserably. So this was what swallowing butterflies felt like. I could hardly stop the giggle from coming out as I typed my response.

Harper: *No one said anything about kissing. Considering you stole the last one, I'm surprised you even asked.*

Cain: *Spontaneous kissing is so much better than permission kissing.*

Harper: *I think any kind of kissing with you is dangerous.*

Cain: *Now* dangerous *is the best kind of kissing. I think your mouth would agree with me there.*

I'm lying on my bed, and I flip over in a fit of giddiness. He is so brazen.

Cain: *You still there or did I make you blush so hard that you had to put the phone down?*

Harper: *God, you're cocky. I'm not discussing this. Thank your lucky stars I'm even letting you take me to this party.*

Cain: *Be ready for a wild night ;)*

I didn't text back after that, too amped up and nervous at the same time to respond. I didn't want to ask too many questions or seem overeager, although I definitely was.

Clothes were thrown about my room, most of them Mary-Kate's. She'd loaned me a few shirts, a jean skirt, a pair of extremely short white shorts, and a dress that was cute. I think the dress was more my speed than any of them, but it would be a game time decision.

MK had delivered them last night before she went to cheer at the game, which I heard the football team won. Not that I was listening on the radio or anything. And not that I let out a little whoop every time Cain threw a touchdown.

My friend had left me with a pat on the ass, winked at me, and told me she couldn't wait to watch me show up to the party with Mr. Popular. I had rolled my eyes at her, but smiled as I closed the door.

Cain was picking me up at eight thirty. Which meant I had two and a half hours to fuss over myself, something I normally wouldn't do. But this was my first official date. If you could consider going to get wasted by a bonfire a date.

I'm about to get in the shower, when I hear something in the kitchen.

Mom is humming, and I know that things with this new guy are going well. She always hums when she's in a new, perfect relationship. Mostly, she'll hum lovey-dovey Sinatra songs under her breath. The question is, how long will the humming last?

I hope it's for real. I hope the men in Haven are more reliable than the ones she dated in the Keys, but who knows? Normally, her humming wouldn't last past a month.

"What're you doing?" I hear Grandma's voice, and I round the corner to peer in on the two of them.

They're side by side at the kitchen counter, preparing dinner, and I can't help but smile. I can see that both of them are making more of an effort to be kind to each other, to perhaps repair their broken relationship.

"Humming a lovely tune," Mom says as she continues to chop an item of food that I can't see.

Grandma is standing over the stove, stirring a pot that contains what smells like chili. "What song is that?"

Mom scoops up what she's chopping and walks it over to the pot, dumping it in while her own mama stirs. "'*I've Got You Under my Skin*' by Frank Sinatra."

My grandmother sighs, and I see a small smile creep onto her face. "Your father loved that song."

Mom looks at her back where she stands by the stove, a quick grin piercing her lips. And, as if nothing has transpired between them over the years, she goes to her. Loops her arms around her shoulders, her front to Grandma's back. She sways her own mother, humming, until Grandma joins in.

The two of them gently shift from foot to foot, quietly singing the tune together, as they cook dinner. And silently, I send up a prayer to the universe that this relationship lasts. That this guy is the forever guy.

Because seeing my mother so happy that she can get along with her mother? Yeah, I could get used to that.

The next two hours go by in a blur of dinner, trying to put some curls in my pin-straight hair, trying on everything in my room and practicing my smile in the mirror. God, I look like an idiot.

I settle on the dress, a flowy maroon mid-length number with tiny wildflowers printed all over it. It shows enough cleavage for even my chest still to be modest, but it's pretty and summery for this Texas heat. I throw a sweater in the bag I'm bringing, along with breath mints, my house keys, a granola bar and my phone and headphones. Who knows what this will be like? Maybe I'll need supplies.

By eight twenty, I'm standing in the front hallway, pacing back and forth and going to the window beside the front door anytime I hear a noise. The anticipation of when Cain will come rumbling down the long gravel driveway is killing me. I feel like I might shout from the rooftops or run to the bathroom to puke. All at the same time.

At three minutes past eight thirty, headlights shine in the distance, and I can hear the booming Blake Shelton song singing out from his speakers.

"Bye!" I call out to Mom and Grandma before they can come out and start talking to him. Or worse, ask us questions about what we are.

I try to walk casually down the stairs, feeling those green eyes all over me. Climbing up into his Jeep feels like I'm getting into a chariot.

"Hey, darlin'," Cain drawls, and I can't take my own eyes off of him.

Dressed in worn blue jeans and a soft white T-shirt, sitting in his open top, he looks like some kind of rugged catalog model. His black hair is windblown, and in the setting sun, I can make out the strong jaw that leads to the lips that attacked mine just a week ago.

"What, no quotes for me?" I tease him, feeling bold.

One eyebrow raises as he pulls out from the front of the ranch. He reaches over, splaying a big palm on the exposed skin of my leg where my dress has risen. "I think I can woo you just fine without relying on my literary friends."

Yeah, he's not kidding.

He leaves his hand on my leg for a majority of the drive. It's possessive, and his skin against mine burns in the best way possible. I shouldn't let him paw me like this, show his dominance, but the embers scorching low in my belly make me forget about correcting him.

I had told myself that I wasn't going to let Cain Kent get to me. But really, I never stood a chance. I could say it was the naïve virgin in me, or that I was weak to his charm.

But ... and this was going to sound even more cliché ... it felt cosmic. I felt as if Cain had shown me a side of himself that he hadn't shown anyone else in Haven. How could it be possible that he'd quote different novels to anyone else? He didn't even know about my writing and he'd done that.

We pull up to a throng of trees, and Cain drives through them. The headlights show over a dirt road, with random fencing and broken gates that we speed past.

Where are we going? "Why do I get the feeling that we are going wherever we are going alone?"

Cain grins over at me. "Nah, although you'd like that, wouldn't you?"

He winks at me, and my heart flip-flops. Another minute or two, and a building comes into view. It's large, an almost warehouse-type hanger in the middle of nowhere. And as I look closer at it, I can see lights twirling around inside. Cain pulls the truck into a field a few yards away, and the music replaces the rumble of the tires on the gravel. A Florida Georgia Line song pulses through the night, and I can now see the hordes of teens spilling out of this building.

"Welcome to The Atrium." Cain comes up beside me, slinging an arm around my shoulder.

But before I can even step foot in this mysterious building he calls The Atrium, Annabelle, the princess of Haven High School, marches directly over to me. "Tell your slut mother to stay away from my father."

My heart skips a beat, falters, and then starts racing. My mouth goes dry, and Cain's arm feels too heavy on me now. "What?"

"You heard me. Tell your whore of a mother to keep her grubby little hands off of my father. He's way too good for her, and we all know she's only after his money." Annabelle practically spits at me, her brown eyes full of alcohol and fury.

I had only been at this party for all of one minute, and I was already being screamed at like an outcast. "My mom ... the guy she's dating is *your* dad?"

I almost can't believe it, so I have to say it out loud. For the past month or so, Mom has been dating Annabelle's dad. This couldn't get any worse.

And just like that, I wish that Mom would stop her humming. That the display I saw in the kitchen earlier would stop ... even if it does make Mom happy. I can't be on Annabelle Mills shit list.

"Yeah, trailer trash. *My* dad. And yeah, I know that you come from some parking lot dump. Makes sense now, you living in a trailer. Take your trashy mother and stay far away from my family."

Someone grabs her slim arm and she shakes them off with a

whip of her brunette mane. And then she walks off, forgetting about me and shaking her arms as someone proposes she shotgun a beer.

She just called me out, in front of everyone, and thank God it's dark because the skin on my cheeks is probably the color of cherries. Trailer trash. That's what she'd said. So someone had told her where I'd come from. And she'd told everyone else.

I duck my head, swiping at the angry, hot tears popping out of my lids.

Tonight was supposed to be what teenage dreams were made of. It was supposed to be magical, butterfly-inducing, a chance to spend the night at Cain's side. But I was a moron. I didn't fit here, as was evident. I didn't operate like these kids

In the first five minutes, Annabelle Mills had brought the paper castle she'd been imagining straight down into the Texas dirt.

And if I was being honest with myself, somewhere deep inside, I had a sinking feeling that Cain was the one who set this whole thing up.

17

CAIN

Typically, if a girl started crying at a party, I'd dump her where she stood and go find a beer and a willing set of tits.

Harper swipes at her eyes, the guys and girls around us going back to their party and forgetting about the scene Annabelle just caused.

She scoots out from beneath my arm, her slim shoulders leaving a tattoo of warmth on my skin that I miss when she pulls away.

"Gotta build a thicker skin here in Texas, darlin'," I drawl, trying to brush off the war of words I just witnessed.

But the advice just comes off dickish, and Harper's blue eyes go wide before she turns on her heel and stalks away from me. I shouldn't care, if she wants to have a bitch fit about mean girls, I should just go into one of my favorite places in Haven and just forget about this.

I should go in there and find a girl who will fuck me in my open-top Jeep, add number ten to my list and win this competition.

But for some stupid fucking reason beyond my comprehension, I follow her. Who knows, maybe I'll comfort her and she'll fall right on my cock. Said cock stirs at the thought of her tight, untouched pussy clenching around me.

Shit, what the hell was I getting myself into with this girl?

"Wait up, woman ..." I half-heartedly jog after her, my legs taking me to her in three long strides.

"You orchestrated this, didn't you? Couldn't wait to humiliate me in front of your crowd. What was it? Payback for that first day in class? God, I'm an idiot." Harper whirls around and begins walking away again.

If I was being truthful, setting a girl up to embarrass her would be something in my wheelhouse. And having someone humiliate her just so I could look like the knight in shining armor when I went to comfort her was a genius move.

But, I hadn't planned this. Although it would work to my advantage, when I convinced her it wasn't me who had fed Annabelle information. Her mom was dating Michael Mills? How ... odd.

"Harper ..." I follow her, the beat of the country music booming out of The Atrium lowering the farther I get away from it.

"Stay away from me." She doesn't turn around.

"I don't care that you lived in a trailer park. Or that your mom is dating her dad." I'm playing on the things that make her self-conscious.

But instead of a silent pat on the back for using my best strategy to get her to sleep with me, I feel a twinge of guilt. That was such an asshole way to say it.

She stops in her tracks, now back by where I parked the truck with nowhere to go. "Is there a cab company in this goddamn forsaken town?"

"You're not taking a cab." I chuckle. "And no, there isn't one if you even wanted to. Uber doesn't exactly exist out here in the country, darlin'."

"I knew you were no good. I knew that you were just fucking with me," she grumbles, looking off into the distance.

Harper has her slim arms crossed and wrapped around her body, as if she's trying to hug and comfort herself. I tentatively move toward the Jeep, toward her.

"I promise you, I had nothing to do with that. Anna ... she has her own issues. With life, this town, and with me. And I apologize that those got taken out on you. But you have to believe me, I wanted nothing more than to have a great time with you tonight."

It wasn't a lie. I did want to have a good time. She doesn't protest when I walk closer to her, and unwind her arms with my hands. I dwarf her, my body and frame so much bigger than her pixie form. It's arousing.

My hands rub up and down her arms, leaving trails of goose bumps in their wake.

"I want to trust you." Those wide, naïve eyes search my face.

That's the exact opposite of what you should do, I think.

But instead, I say, "You should trust me."

Harper doesn't speak again, and after a beat, I lead her to the truck. The backseat of it.

I can feel her heart rate spike under my fingers, the ones that are laced with my own. My own pulse is roaring in my ears. I'm not sure why. Sure, I get a stiffy when I know I'm about to get laid, maybe my balls draw up tight. But my heart, the most vulnerable muscle in the body, never moves. Not even a twitch.

We climb up into my Jeep, and I angle Harper, setting the scene for her because I know she doesn't know what to do.

Before she can overthink anything, I lean in and kiss her. Gently at first, to get her into the groove of things. My lips slide against hers, the rumble of arousal stealing over my muscles like the edge of a knife gliding along steel. Opening, I tentatively join our tongues, and growl when Harper moans into my mouth.

Her moan spurs me to action, my tongue diving deeper and the kiss becoming *more*. Grabbing her waist, I shift her, practically pick her up in the air and plant her in my lap. The cute sundress, something innocent among the crop tops and booty shorts here tonight, splays over her thighs. It rides up and leaves room for my hands to roam her naked flesh.

I don't care that I'm missing the party that I'm supposed to be putting on.

I don't care that I'm not even participating in the debauchery that I was so keyed up to enjoy tonight.

I don't care that it feels better than it should. Deeper, more exciting, my emotions twisting in with something that should be purely physical.

I don't care that I'm almost coming in my pants just from the thought of touching her tits.

The only thing I care about is that Harper is straddling my lap. That she's letting me touch her.

"Cain …" Harper breaks off the kiss, and I might have spoken too soon. "I … I want to, keep going. But … I haven't done this."

The moonlight pours into the backseat, and I look her in the eyes. "We'll go slow."

Normally, I would charm the female sitting in my lap. I would push them just a little bit, make them feel euphoria with my fingers, all just to get my cock in their pants. But the words leave my mouth and I know for a fact that I won't break that promise. I try to tell myself it's all part of my master plan, that I'll entice her in like a fly to my spider's web. I'll be nice, gentle, slow … until she's all the way in and I can pounce on my prey.

This time, she's the one who leans back in for the kiss. Her small hands explore my jaw, tickling, feeling. Our mouths do that languid, hot dance, all time stopped or speeding … it was hard to tell which way was up. It took a lot for me to get lost in just kissing, and yet, I could not use my five senses for anything else but Harper Posy.

My hands knead at the soft skin of her thighs, not too high to reach her underwear under her dress, but high enough to make her gasp into my mouth. When my hands make their way up her body, molding to the curves under the material she wears, her fingers trace down. We meet in the middle, tracing patterns over the other's chest as I bite playfully at her bottom lip.

Taking the plunge, I round second base. My fingers slip the skinny straps off of her shoulders, to find that she isn't wearing a bra. My cock pulses at the thought of nothing but the thin cloth of dress between my hands and her gorgeous tits.

Harper has stopped moving her mouth, hovering it there over mine, waiting for me to make a move. She isn't protesting, so I gently shove the straps down. Down, down, down, so that they take the triangles of material over her breasts with them.

I move back a fraction, my head hitting the headrest behind me.

There she sits, atop my lap, in the moonlight. Her breasts are more than a handful each, and her nipples, rosy and flushed, are hard and budded under my gaze.

"You're a sight." I bring a hand up, biting my knuckles because she's so fucking sexy.

So innocent, so beautiful, so womanly even. And untouched, that's the best part. Mine to conquer first, like an explorer setting his flag on new land.

I don't do anything that night in the truck but make out with Harper and roll her nipples and tits in my hands. But I would be lying if I said it wasn't the most exciting hookup I'd had in four years.

18

HARPER

If smoking pot at a beach bonfire is the Florida thing, then hanging out on the river is the Texas thing.

Half of Haven High School seems to be parked along the shoulder of the road as Mary-Kate pulls her truck into the long line of pickups. She stops the car, grabs her bag, and starts to get out.

"Um, where are we going?" We aren't anywhere close to ... well, anywhere.

MK laughs and points. "That clearing up there, we have to walk about five minutes into the woods until we get to the river."

I bristle, thinking this seems like a bad idea. But it is the middle of the afternoon, and even though it's November, it's still almost eighty degrees outside.

I shouldn't even be going to this thing after last night. After I let Cain touch me in places that no boy has ever touched me before. After I let him wipe away my tears, and tell me everything I wanted to hear.

Had he been lying? It sure didn't feel like it. And when he'd dropped me off at home, an hour later than my curfew so I had to sneak through my bedroom window, he'd planted a gentle kiss on my lips.

Aside from the Annabelle debacle, last night had been perfect. And I flushed inside every time I thought about Cain and me in that backseat. Which was only, oh, every damn second.

I follow her, gripping my bag to my side as we walk through brush and trees, most definitely getting poison ivy in the process.

"This better be worth it," I grumble.

"Trust me, it's a good time. Plus, you told me you wanted to see all of Haven, so I'm giving you the grand tour." MK winks at me.

"That was when I was being open and fun. Now I'm dirty and sweating," I grumble again, and she shakes her butt at me as we break through the trees.

Then my mouth drops. Kids in the water, on the banks, hanging from rope swings and up on a train bridge that looks like it hasn't seen a locomotive in what looks like fifty years. Music is blaring, red cups are everywhere, and every person here is in a bathing suit. Floats fill the water, coolers crowd the sand and I almost can't believe that no one can hear this from the shoulder of the road where we left our car.

I sure hadn't heard it.

"You want to jump first and then we can lay out and get a tan?" Mary-Kate is sliding her bag off of her shoulder and onto the sand, stripping down to only her bikini.

I feel self-conscious. Even though I lived in a bathing suit as a Florida native, something about Haven and its teenagers made me doubt my body. I was fully aware that my boobs fell out of any top I purchased, and my simple black two piece was nothing compared to these girls and their designer swimwear.

Backing up so that I'm almost against the trees, I shrug out of my shorts and tank top, and set my bag behind a big oak so that no one can take it. When I reveal myself, MK whistles at me and a bunch of people look. I must blush the color of a ripe strawberry.

"Let's go!" She claps and I follow her, folding my arms across my body as we walk.

My skin bristles and I know he's here. *Cain*. Is it strange that I am fully aware whenever he's in my presence now, even if I don't see him?

He hadn't told me he was going to be here, but did he have to? After last night, what was the protocol? I was all so new to this.

Immediately, MK wants to jump off of the old looking bridge. Apparently, it's what everyone does. A rite of passage.

Which is why, ten minutes after that, I'm teetering on the edge of said bridge, at least fifty or sixty kids splashing in the water below or horsing around on the bridge beside me while chanting at me to jump.

My legs shake, and I'm petrified. This has to be about a forty-foot drop. While it doesn't look so high when you're driving up to it, standing on the precipice is another story. It's not the act of doing it that seizes me, it's the fear. The mental lock on my brain that tells me no, you cannot move your limbs to accomplish this.

Suddenly, the bridge starts to shake, and I let out a yelp.

"Don't freak out," A deep voice says beside me.

I turn my head, and there is Cain, naked save for a pair of white and navy plaid board shorts. Momentarily, my fear skedaddles and lust replaces it. Lord have mercy, this guy is hot. Six-pack abs, long, lean arms and legs, that strong jaw. His olive skin and jet-black hair are already wet, meaning he must have seen me from the water and came up here.

"Wh-what are you doing?" I can't help but stutter, both from the lust and the fear.

"Making sure you're okay." His small smile has my heart galloping.

"This is higher than it looks." We're standing close, his hand right next to mine, gripping the cables behind us.

"It's not as bad as it seems ... and once you jump, the feeling is indescribable."

Kind of like standing on this bridge with you, I think.

"But, the water ... it's not deep enough." I put up another excuse.

Cain raises an eyebrow. "You know it is. You saw dozens of kids do it before. Don't let your brain mess with you."

His eyes skate my body, and a chill of goose bumps breaks out even though it's hot and muggy. I bite my lip, and he stares at the motion. People are staring at us now, I can see them point to us from down in the water.

"I'll hold your hand. And on the count of three, we jump." He nods as if to get me to agree.

Holding out his big, calloused palm, I inspect it for a second. My fear is dissipating, and the need to touch him grows stronger. I grasp it, sucking in my breath for a second as my hand comes off the cable of the bridge. Now I'm teetering with just one hand grasping the structure behind me, the blood in my knuckles turning cold.

I hesitate for a split second before lacing my fingers through his. Our hands are no match for each other; his is big, brawny and tan, mine is small, delicate and pale. But he grips the only part of me he can hold onto as if I've just given him a gift, and my mouth goes dry feeling the roughness of his skin against my own palm.

Cain's full bottom lip is now between his teeth, and I've never wanted to kiss a boy more than I do right now.

"Okay, on the count of three, we're going to jump. Got it?" He squeezes my hand.

I'm too scared about the jump and enamored by him to talk, so I nod, taking a deep breath as he counts off.

"Three!" Cain shouts, and before I know it, I'm letting go of the bridge behind me and pushing off hard with my legs, my toes hitting the open air last.

Cain's hand is plastered to mine, his body drifting toward me as we drop. It's like we're in slow motion; I look at the water below, the sky above, and then over to him. He's watching me, a genuine smile stretching his face. I smile back, a giggle escaping my mouth.

This feeling is ... everything. The falling, the leap of my heart, the way my toes wiggle through the open air.

What hits my heart most of all was that Cain climbed out there with me. He showed everyone in the river and on its banks that we were ... what? Together? In spite of my knowledge not to think wishfully, I did it anyway. I hope we are together.

When we finally hit the water, it burns. In the best way possible.

19

CAIN

The tiny marina on McCray Lake houses less than a dozen decent sized boats, and maybe ten little dinghies.

Gnats buzz in clusters around the humid, musty water, and the brush and cattails hide the lake from the outside world. I sit on the hood of my Jeep in my fishing gear, my tackle box on the ground next to me.

I see a Camry with a Hook & Hunt logo sticker slapped on the side pull up, and Harper's eyes dance with laughter when she sees who is waiting for their fishing lesson.

"You booked me to be your caddy of fishing?" She smirks as she gets out of the car, worn jean shorts and a plain white tank top looking way too good on her.

"I figured you needed a little break from the office." I push off the truck and walk to her, not stopping until my hands are in her hair and my mouth is exploring hers.

Harper gives a little squeak and a moan, and I'm hard as a steel pipe in two seconds flat. I'm usually raring to go, but this girl does something else entirely to me.

I'm not sure what the fuck I'm doing. Why I'm pursuing this

girl so hard. And I really need to stop thinking of her as "this girl," because I repeat the name Harper in my head so many times a day that I should really stop lying to myself.

I know better than this. The females in my life always leave. My mother couldn't even stand to be around me, and I don't need psychoanalysis to realize that's why I can't form a lasting bond with anyone of the opposite gender.

But Harper ... she makes all of those fears and self-doubts disappear when I'm with her. How does she do that? And why am I letting her?

We'd seen each other in school, had smirked when we passed each other or shared a flirty word. But I'd been busy with practice and I knew Harper wasn't going to make a move. I could see it in her eyes, she wanted to experiment more. So did I, not that it would happen on the boat today. She wasn't the kind of girl who would let me get her naked on the open water, but hell if my cock didn't know how fucking hot that would be.

Yes, if we form a relationship and she falls for me, and lets me take her to bed ... then I'm accomplishing my end goal. I wanted to get close to her, to fuck her. That was my original mission.

But what if it came at a cost? What if I was falling too? I didn't want that shit, didn't need those feelings. Girlfriends were something I didn't do, especially now when I was going to graduate and go off to college. I had no time for romance and fights and caring ... college football was a full-time career.

But here I was, paying her place of work for fishing lessons that I didn't need purely so I could spend more time with her. I knew what Grady and the guys would say. I was pussy whipped. That a girl was getting the best of me. They'd been curious about our time spent together, wanted to know where I had gone last weekend at The Atrium.

It wasn't technically a practice day, but on Sunday most of the seniors met at the school weight room to shoot the shit and work our muscles.

"Kent, where did you get off to last night?" Emmitt throws a barbell off his shoulders and to the ground.

Grady sits up from the bench he's doing chest presses on, and asks the same. "Yeah, I barely even saw you! You missed the two topless sophomores who lost in beer pong."

"Aw damn, can't say I wouldn't have liked to see that. But I had other ... matters to attend to."

"What he means by matters is that new girl, Harper." Paul smirks.

I shrug, not giving away any details. I want them to think I'm putting my hands all over that girl. I have a reputation to uphold.

"Too bad you haven't fucked her." Grady's jealousy seethes through as he bumps me on his way to the water fountain.

"How do you know?" I pick up a medicine ball and start throwing it against a wall, and catching it on the bounce back.

"Because you'd be bragging like a king. You'd have won. No one would keep their tenth girl a secret. Unless ... you were falling for her or some shit." Emmitt eyes me.

Will has been silent for most of this ridiculous conversation, as he usually always is. But even he perks up at Emmitt's last sentence.

Six pairs of eyes are glued to me. I fix up my face before I turn around from where I am facing the wall, putting on my superstar quarterback golden boy persona.

"Believe me, she doesn't mean jack shit to me. Just another pair of tits and ass. But this one needs hand holding before she spreads her legs. Don't worry, I'll beat you fuckers."

I try to keep that sentiment in mind, ignore the throbbing of my heart in my chest as I pull back from Harper and she looks up at me with a radiant smile.

"Do you really not know how to fish?" She tilts her head.

I put a fingertip on her chin. "Sweetheart, I'm a boy growing up in the boondocks of Texas, close to a lake. Of course I know how to fish. I just wanted to see if you did."

Harper scowls. "You do know that I worked at a bait and tackle shop for like, two years in Florida, right? I bet I'll bag way more fish than you."

"Is that a bet?" It reminds me that she is only a bet, too.

"Nah, I don't want to compete with you. Fishing is supposed to be relaxing. Plus, I think you play too many games as it is." She pins me with those baby blues.

I follow her down the dock, carrying her tackle box like the gentleman I am. Because I paid for this fishing lesson, we get to use the store's boat, which is a little nicer than the crappy old dinghy my dad had always taken me on. Once we're all set up, our lines in the water, sitting next to each other in the bucket seats, she turns to me.

"You've lived in Haven your whole life?"

I nod. "Born and raised. Third generation."

"So, are your grandparents and parents around?"

I grin at her. "What is this, twenty questions? My gramps is in a nursing home right off Main Street. My dad is in the military, so he's not around a lot."

She doesn't ask about my mom, so she must have heard about it from somewhere. "That must be hard. So ... it's just you? Do you live with anyone? A teammate's family?"

My line begins to pull, and I try to reel it in, but whatever I caught wriggles free. I sit back again. "Nope, just me and my lonesome in my dad's house. I'm eighteen, so legally I'm allowed to live alone. It gets real quiet though. Maybe you can come over and keep me company."

Harper glances at me, trying to maintain the blush on her cheeks. "Somehow, I think that would be very dangerous for me."

I play innocent, brushing a lock of hair off her shoulder. "What? I just want you to come over to see my bookcase."

She turns her whole body to me, folding her long, slim legs under her. "What's with that? You just happen to like to read and know all of these passages from classic books? And why do I feel like I'm the only one who knows this factoid?"

I sigh. Normally, I hide my interest for books. Girls don't care about that shit, they'd rather hear about football or kiss you. And my friends would call me a pussy. But, Harper, she's genuinely interested.

"My granny, God rest her soul, got me into it. After my mom skipped town, she kind of become my surrogate mama. This one summer, she'd read a paperback every two days out by the blow up pool she set up in her backyard for me. I loved her like hell, and wanted to imitate her. I was about ten, and she'd told me that if I wanted to do it right, I'd pick a better book than *When You Give a Mouse a Cookie*. She'd gone to the library and checked out *The Adventures of Huckleberry Finn*, and I was hooked. I read, I think, about eight books that summer. More than I'd ever read in my entire life probably, in three months. After that, I'd ask for copies of my own for every birthday and Christmas."

Harper's eyes light up. "God, I would love to have my own bookcase of copies."

I stare at her. "You like to read so much, I assume, since you are always bugging me about my books. You're telling me you don't have any books at home?"

She shakes her head. "No room for books in a trailer, remember? And, not really much money left over after other expenses. I was a library kid."

"You were the little girl sitting between the stacks, weren't you?" I could just see her, knobby knees with stacks of books she wanted to read piling up around her.

Chuckling, Harper nods. "So, what are you reading now?"

My line jiggles, and I grab hold of it. Harper's does too, and our attention goes to the rods in the water. "I'm re-reading *Jurassic Park* before the next movie comes out."

Harper makes a humming sound in the back of her throat, concentrating on reeling in her catch. She's struggling, and I let go of whatever is on the end of my line, moving behind her where she now stands to help her pull. Her body is flush against mine, and I smell the daisy scent in her hair.

We pull together, her cute little grunts filling the air. Finally, we've got the fish up and on deck.

"She's a beauty." Harper beams, staring down at her catch.

She nabbed a foot long trout, and she's right, it's a nice fish.

"Guess I did beat you." She smirks, and her eyebrows raise.

Oh, sweetheart, if you only knew how much further behind me you actually were. I just pray she doesn't catch on to what game we are actually playing.

20

HARPER

Cain: *I can't stop thinking about your tits.*

Holy hell.

I couldn't stop thinking about him touching them. Since that night at The Atrium, we hadn't done more than kiss. Although I was not sad about how that night had ended, I did wish I'd seen more of the mysterious party place that was whispered about in reverence through the halls of Haven High School.

Mary-Kate had been miffed that I hadn't checked in with her when I got there, but as soon as I'd told her what had happened in hushed words, she'd squealed and forgiven me. However, she had told me I'd missed a wild night in the building that had been an army depot during World War II. That would have been cool to see, but I liked what I'd done better.

Every time I thought about Cain touching me in the moonlight, heat would pool between my legs. I wanted to do it again, every time I saw him. Just thinking his name brought excitement, and I now understood why sex was so addicting. I hadn't even had it yet, but each time I thought of Cain Kent, I pictured getting naked with him and having our bodies meet. Everywhere.

Harper: *You're making me blush.*

Cain: *I want to see you blush everywhere. It turns me on.*

He was being so blunt, and I squeezed my thighs together where I lay on the bed. Were we sexting? I'd never sexted before, and it made me giddy.

Harper: *I turn you on?*

Cain: *More than you know. Want me to show you?*

I'm pretty sure he's asking if I want him to send me a dick pic, and the answer is a hard no.

Harper: *You know I've never been with anyone, right? I think that's a little too fast for my speed.*

I might be putting a damper on the sexting, but if I was going to see him naked, I wanted it to be in person the first time. I wasn't as technology obsessed as my age would portray me as.

Cain: *I know, I know, we're taking it slow. But let me just tell you, you drive me wild, baby.*

I flush at the word baby. This boy could make me turn red as a ripe, juicy apple about to fall hard to the ground from its secure, but safe, branch.

Harper: *I don't know how to do this, but ...*

Cain: *Stop thinking. Tell me what you want me to do to you.*

I squeal. I can't believe I am actually going to do this.

Harper: *I want you to kiss me. Like you did that night in the car. Slow and searching.*

Cain: *I'll do more than kiss you.*

Harper: *And I want you to feel me again.*

Cain: *That was one of the hottest night's I've ever had.*

Harper: *But you've had many, right?*

I couldn't help the self-doubt creeping in. He'd probably done that dozens of times with other girls. In the exact same location, the same backseat of his car.

Cain: *None of that matters. What happened in the past doesn't matter. You're the only one, Harper.*

Does he say that to all of the girls? Or does he really mean that? Can I trust what I'd seen in his eyes that night at The Atrium.

And speaking of the night at The Atrium, there was something I needed to discuss with Mom. I leave my phone on my bed, not sure how to respond to Cain. I am never truly sure how to talk to him ... sometimes he seems larger than life. So I go to seek out Mom, to talk to her about what else happened that night.

I find her on the deck out back, drinking a glass of wine and scribbling on notepads. I can tell she's doing something for work, for her students, or for the principal to look over.

"Mom, how come you didn't tell me you were dating Mr. Mills?" I broach the subject carefully, but dive right into it, knowing I need to get this off my chest.

She turns around from where she's lesson planning at the table. "How do you know Michael?"

I bite the inside of my cheek. "I don't know him, I know his daughter."

She slaps her forehead and puts down her pen. "Of course you do, I completely forgot that he had a daughter in the same grade as you."

"Yeah, and she just happens to be the homecoming queen." I roll my eyes.

"Oh, Harper, I'm sure she's lovely."

Should I tell my mom that said lovely girl called her a whore not more than two weeks ago?

"Believe me, Mom, she's not. Do you really like this guy? Because if it's just another one of your boyfriends, can you end it now? On my behalf?"

It's probably selfish of me to ask this of her, and I know I'm being kind of irrational giving in to this peer pressure, but I've had to endure years of her men bullshit. The least she could is sacrifice one relationship for me. I mean, I did move across state lines because one of those dating adventures ended badly.

She blinks at me. "Harper ... wow. That is so ... selfish of you. No, I will not stop seeing him. I really like Michael, and I think ... this could be it."

"You say that every time," I grumble, thinking of how I can plead with her.

I hear something slam, and when I look over, the expression in Mom's eyes is pure hurt. "So what if I'm a romantic? I've said it before and I'll say it again; If believing too much in love is my worst quality, then you should be damn happy to have me as a mother. And you know what? Yes, I realize that sometimes my relationships affect you, but I've always put you first. We moved here for your quality of life, not because I had a bad breakup. I knew that a senior year at Haven could give you more than we ever had in Florida. You would have a family, albeit small, here.

The school was better, the town was better. We would live in an actual house, with your very own bedroom."

She stops, wiping at her eyes which are now shining with tears. "I raised you as a single mother, which isn't something I want a pat on the back for, but you need to realize that I've done everything for you. I would do it every day, for the rest of my life ... but when it comes to who I date, I'm sorry but you don't get a say. Unless it's harmful to me, which Michael is the complete opposite of, then you don't get to tell me that I have to break up with him. He makes me happy, he's a good man. If you don't want to be friends with his daughter, then fine. But he is the first man since your father ..."

Mom breaks off, choking on a sob. I can see how much I've upset her, and I am quick to get up, to wrap my arms around her neck.

"Never mind. I'm sorry I said anything. I want you to be happy." I shush her, wiping a tear.

My heart sinks for having put demands on her. She was right. We didn't have the most glamorous life, but she'd always provided for me. Kept the house clean. Done my homework with me and made sure that dinner was on the table and that Friday night always held a movie and popcorn. She's a good mother, and if dating is her one vice, I will have to live with it.

Even if Annabelle Mills maims me in the process.

21

HARPER

Typically, I enjoy writing outside.

The fresh air, the sun or the moon, just me and the landscape. In Florida, I would head to the beach with my computer. But here in Haven, I have acres in my very own backyard.

However, for the past week or so, I'd had such bad writer's block that any time I picked up my laptop, my brain would go blank. I'd tried it all; plotting exercises, re-reading chapters I'd already drafted, checking out a book from the library just to read for pleasure. And none of it had worked.

So today, I decided on a change of venue. While most of Main Street in Haven was compromised of the typical small town necessity shops—a dry cleaner, a dive bar, the post office—there was one decent coffee shop. It played acoustic cafe music, had worn wood tables, and a pretty good vanilla latte. And most importantly, it was quiet and dim-lighted ... the perfect haven in Haven to write.

I've gotten in a solid thousand words, which makes me want to weep with joy, when I gaze off, looking out the big plate glass window I'm sitting next to. It gives a picturesque view out onto the main drag, and since moving here I've begun to appreciate the charm of a small southern town. Not that where I was from in Florida was any big city, but something about Haven just felt so inclusive and down home. Everyone knew everyone, there was a pride about being from here.

As I gaze out the window, I suddenly spot Cain across the street. He's walking with his hands in his pockets, a Haven football sweatshirt thrown over a pair of jeans. It isn't necessarily chilly at sixty degrees, but people from warm places have a different opinion of what cold is.

I watch him, wondering where he is going or coming from. His black hair is blowing in the wind, the hard planes of his olive-skinned face so beautiful in the streetlights.

He's standing under one, looking across the street, straight at me but not seeing me. I stare at him, a small smile spreading my lips. The kind of smile that forms when you see someone but they don't see you, the kind of smile you have the second their mind clicks into place and they notice you looking at them.

Cain sees me, and his eyebrow raises, as if to ask how long I'd been staring at him. I raise a hand and wave, and he starts over toward the coffee shop.

I try to slyly check my appearance in the computer screen that's gone black in my absence, but I feel those green eyes on me. Looking up, there he stands.

"Hey, gorgeous." Cain slides into the empty seat across from mine.

"Well, hello. What're you doing tonight?" I can't control my jiggling knee or the nerves lighting up my stomach like fireflies.

"I was just visiting my gramps at his nursing home around the corner. What brings you here?" Cain picks up the last piece of chocolate croissant on my discarded plate and pops it in his mouth.

"Just wanted to get out of the house." I shrug, not wanting to get into what I was actually doing.

But, like everything else in his universe, what Cain wants to know or see just simply presents itself. He slides the computer away from me and wiggles the touchpad on the keyboard, turning the screen to him.

"Hey!" I protest, trying to grab it back.

He *tsks* at me and brings the laptop onto his knees, where I can't reach it. For a minute or two, Cain's eyes study the screen.

"Is this ... did you write this?" He looks at me, curious.

He's seen the program I write in, that lays out books in chapters and sections.

"Yes." I blink, not knowing what he thinks and not wanting to say more.

"You're writing a book? An honest-to-God book?" Cain's mouth is breaking out into a grin.

"I am. But ... well it's only a first draft and it's not done and I'm not even sure what I'm doing ..." I start to ramble.

He sets my laptop down, leans across the table, and kisses me full on the mouth. "I think that's pretty damn cool, darlin'. What's it about? When will you finish it and can I read it?"

My mouth hangs open, because honestly, I hadn't even seriously thought about anyone reading my book. Yes, I'd thought of the aspects of publishing, how to do it, when, the mechanics of it. But I hadn't truly thought about someone actually reading my words. It made my whole body convulse with nervous energy at once.

"It's a thriller, a suspense fiction novel. I ... I have probably about five chapters left to go and then it will be finished." I didn't answer his question about reading it.

"And when can I read it?" Cain tries to grab for my computer again, but like a ninja, I take it, save my work and slip it into my backpack.

"I'm not sure. Maybe I'll make you buy it like everyone else."

"Only if you sign it for me. I'll tell everyone that I made out with you when you're a famous author." His fingers seek my palm and he begins rubbing his thumb in small circles around it.

"I'll think about," I say, flirting with him.

"When did you start doing this?" he asks.

"About a year and a half ago. You know about my love for books. One day I just decided to start playing around with writing. And the idea that I had just kept developing, and I couldn't stop. It's what I want to do. I want to travel the world with nothing but my laptop and the ideas in my head."

It sounded so wistful, such a pipe dream. But Cain surprises me by saying, "I think that if that's your dream, you should pursue it full force. I think you could do anything you wanted."

His words are genuine, and I have to blink at him because without even knowing me that long and without even reading the book, he believes that I can publish it. That I can succeed.

"I'm hungry. Want to go grab a burger?" Cain switches the subject, and a flicker of doubt waves through my brain that he actually did care about my interests.

But, I'd do anything to spend more time with him. "Sure, I'm done writing anyway."

"I know an author ... how cool am I? Come on, Ms. Austen, dinner is on me."

We walk out of the cafe, as the light is disappearing on Main Street. Darkness closes in, and the neon signs of the restaurants and bars glow all along the main drag. Cain links his fingers in mine, and we walk, swinging our conjoined arms like a pair of old, content married people.

An alley comes up on our right, and Cain catches my face in his free hand, his smile curving devilishly. "Be spontaneous with me."

I have no idea what's on his mind, but I can't resist that playful grin.

Cain pulls me into the alley, toward the back and behind some boxes stacked outside from the business whose side door leads out here. Anyone could see us, if they looked hard enough, as they walked by.

He winds his hand in my hair, tugging back a bit so that I look up into his face. "You wanted me to kiss, to touch you. To show you more."

I can barely breathe I am so aroused. I've never felt like this, like I might melt into a puddle of lust right at his feet. All thoughts of dinner are abandoned as I make the move to close the gap between our mouths.

My hands conform to either side of his jaw, angling his head where I need it to be. I'm not sure what's come over me ... maybe it's that I've told him my dream and he encouraged it. Maybe it's that I'm growing more comfortable with him, that we've been doing this flirting dance back and forth like some kind of mating ritual and now it was time to act.

Cain has me pinned to the wall, his lower half grinding into mine as we kiss, our tongues exploring every crevice of the others mouth. My hands move down, gripping the sides of his neck and feeling the sheared hair there. It pricks at my palms and sends a shiver down my spine. They trail his sweatshirt, and I burn to feel what's underneath. I haven't explored much of Cain beneath his clothes. Having no real experience doing so with anyone, I don't want to look like a fool.

As soon as I slip my hand under his clothing and touch the hot slab of stone that makes up his stomach, a growl unfurls in his throat. It travels down my own, our mouths fused. The sound makes my knees wobble, and I'm wet in my underwear. I've never felt this liquid heat sticking to my underwear before.

In my exploration of Cain's body, I hadn't realized that his hands were roaming too. Not until they get to the button on my jeans, working at it.

I splay my fingers on the naked flesh beneath them and push gently. "Cain ..."

His hand stays at my button. "Is this okay?"

I gulp, knowing that I'm about to go into uncharted territory. "Yes."

The word comes out definitively, but in my head, I'm shaking all over.

He flicks it and suddenly it's undone, a move I've done a thousand times over the course of my life but one that no boy has ever done to me. Cain kisses my neck, thrills of electricity striking my spine. The chilled air hits my bare stomach where his hand has inched my shirt up to get better access to my jeans. I don't care though; I'm on fire.

My hands, meanwhile, are skating across the planes of his abs, a light dusting of hair unfurling as I drag them lower, right to the top of his belt. I'm not ready to explore there yet, the thought of it makes me shake with nerves.

And then, as if by some sort of stealthy magic, Cain's fingers are in my underwear. They're stroking the top of my mound, the skin soft and shaved. I had always trimmed it off, because I personally didn't like the feel of the prickly, stubbly hair. Cain must like this, because he's growling as he sinks his teeth into my neck. It makes my knees wobble again, and I have to grab onto his hips under his sweatshirt to keep myself upright.

I moan into his mouth, aware that the alley echoes and anyone could walk past and find us. Cain responds with his own lustful noise and I feel like I might explode into a million tiny pieces of iridescent pleasure. His fingers are so close now, brushing down, exploring skin, until ...

Oh. God.

One large digit brushes me there, the bundle of nerves that

is taut and slick. It sends me reeling, has me gasping for breath, trying to grab onto a semblance of thought.

But I can't, I had no idea that this would feel this way. It's like the sun shining directly onto one part of your body. Like an itch you never knew you had to scratch but when you did, the longest sigh imaginable was let out.

Cain rubs in slow circles. So slow that I feel like he must be touching me for years, maybe even decades at a time. I can't breathe there are so many sensations in my body. And then slowly, his finger starts to move under me, away from the dot that was making everything in me tighten.

I must be a useless body right now, not that I care because I'm too focused on where his fingers are going. Suddenly, a sharp pain stabs me.

"Breathe through it, feel my finger inside of you. Feel the fullness," Cain whispers in my ear.

It's only his words, kind of dirty and Zen at the same time, that make me fight past the throbbing discomfort below. And it works. Once I push past that sting, I can feel his finger inside of me.

Inside of me.

He must have popped my cherry. I always thought that was just a metaphor, but I should have done more research to figure out that it actually was a thing. That it would hurt.

But now, it doesn't hurt at all. Cain moves his finger, slowly pumping it in and out of me in shallow strokes, and I groan. This is a different kind of pleasure, deeper than when he was rubbing me.

I can't believe I'm actually letting him finger me in an alley on Main Street. It feels risky and delicious, and so out-of-body because I don't do this. Cain makes me a different person.

"You're beautiful." He breathes, our eyes meeting.

I feel where he's hard, grinding against my leg, our jeans creating friction.

After a while, he pulls his fingers away and kisses me, our tongues tangling once more.

When he pulls away, he says, "Let's go get a burger." And smiles.

I have no idea how I'm supposed to sit across a table from him right now and not blush like crazy, but I don't want to say good night.

I know that I didn't have an orgasm, something in me still feels needy and unanswered, but maybe he thinks I did. Either way, tonight was probably one of the biggest moments of my life. Big in the sense that I would be a different Harper moving forward.

That old me was gone.

22

CAIN

"Take me over there, my regular pew. You know the one, sonny."

Gramps points and I obey, the first mate to his captain on this Sunday exploration. We are at Immaculate Conception Church, the worship capital of Haven. It's packed to the rafters on a Sunday at ten a.m., which of course is the only time Gramps likes to go. He has been coming to this church for seventy years, had been married here, and had watched me be dunked in that baptismal font when I was just a youngster.

Like I said, I'm not a religious man. But that doesn't mean I'm not a respectful southern boy who wouldn't take his gramps to church at the old man's request.

I loop an arm around my grandfather and do as he says, walking slowly as he uses a cane in his other hand to help him hobble to his favorite seat. I smile and nod as we pass familiar faces; Coach and his wife, the woman who owns the diner I frequent with friends, the local radio announcer and his family of six, and Grady and his parents. He looks like a choir boy in his light blue suit jacket. I'll have to make fun of him for that later.

As we take our seats in the pew, I spot a familiar head of long corn silk hair just two rows in front of us.

Beside Harper sits a woman with dark hair down to her shoulders, and on the other side of her is an older woman with a graying, short-cut bob.

Must be her mother and her grandmother. I've encountered Mrs. Posy in town over the years, at church with my grandparents, and have seen her from time to time come out onto her land to observe the early hours of our parties. She seems stoic, Godly, a no-nonsense type of person. I wonder if that was why Harper has come to church, or if she is actually religious.

Drilling holes into her head with my eyes must work, because she turns, her blue pools catching my green ones. I grin at her, wink, and she blushes. I love when that pale, creamy skin tinges pink. Her eyes burn and her strawberry-tinted lips curve up. We're thinking about the same thing ... our night in the alley just days ago.

Fuck, just thinking about it has me semi-hard. In a house of God. I need to think about dead fish or something, but with Harper sitting just feet away from me, it's impossible.

She hadn't even reciprocated that night and it had been ... incredible. I'd never wanted to touch a girl more, to hear her unravel in my ear, to feel her body melt beneath my fingers. Harper was a virgin, now I'd confirmed it by popping her cherry. That was so fucking hot within itself ... but I hoped I'd been gentle enough with her.

Gentle enough?

Since I'd met her, I'd had some kind of fascination with her. And I'd thought that it was because I wanted to spoil her, to take her virginity and add her to my list, like some kind of kinky collector. But I realize now that it's more.

Every time I am with her, whether it's flirting in school or grabbing a bite to eat or hanging out a party ... I want to spend even more time with her. When she trusted me enough to let me touch the most intimate part of her, I felt honored. Not in a sleazy, *I'm going to get to third base*, way, but in a way that meant we trusted each other and I wanted to make her feel good. Pure pleasure, just for her.

Maybe ... I could just forget the initial reason why I'd gone after her. What she never knew wouldn't hurt her. Because from here on out, I want to pursue her, for real. This is beyond rational thought, I don't have the time or maybe even the capacity to fall in love with a girl, but for Harper, I want to be that guy.

Who the fuck was I? Sorry, God, didn't mean to swear on your property.

The service went by agonizingly slow, but I knew Gramps was content with being here and the old man didn't have a lot of good days. I knew this because I was the one who spoke with the staff in my dad's absence, who brought him the Lifesaver candy he requested and got him outside even when he told me sunshine was for suckers.

As the priest gives us his final blessing, parishioners start to file out to the lawn, where an after-service picnic is being held. Everyone in their Sunday best, celebrating the holiness of the day. Yeah right, who were they all kidding? They were here to gossip, bless-their-hearts, and keep up with the latest golden families of Haven.

Gramps is slow going, but I see the Posy trio of women sitting at a table under a big weeping willow tree, and direct him over to it.

"Hello, Blanche, nice to see you," My grandfather greets Harper's grandmother.

She gives him a small smile. "Jacob, I hope you're having a blessed Sunday. And I assume this is the young man who has a golden arm and also seems unable to ring my doorbell when he takes my granddaughter on a date?"

I pale under her scrutinizing gaze, and glance at Harper, who is holding her breath so as not to let out the giggle about to burst out of it.

I extend my hand. "Mrs. Posy, I'm Cain Kent. I apologize about that, next time, I'll remember to bring flowers for your garden."

Gramps is staring at me, his shrewd brows raised. "You best do that. I didn't raise you and your daddy not to be gentlemen."

Harper's mom is staring at me, a huge grin on her face. "Oh, I've so been waiting to meet you. Our girl has been practically giddy, I knew there must be a special boy involved."

"Mom!" Harper groans, embarrassed.

She looks like an angel today, in a white sundress with her hair flowing freely except for the braid wrapping around the crown of her head.

"She's the special one, Ms. Posy." I stick out my hand to her as well, and then hold my hand up to Harper in a quick hello.

What I want to do is steal her away and kiss her silly behind the large trunk of the willow tree, but I refrain, planting my feet to the spot.

"Blanche, he's a charmer, my boy. He's a good egg though, has a great arm. Going to the university a couple towns over next year, gonna be a big star." Gramps beams proudly.

"Harper, why don't you take your charmer and go round us all up some lemonade?" her grandma instructs her, and I have a feeling she wants to grill my grandfather for more information about me.

My heart didn't thump like it used to when I thought I was doing something wrong where it came to Harper. Maybe God had absolved me. Maybe it was because I'd decided, in that church, to pursue her correctly. To actually follow through on a relationship.

Maybe that's why my heart was no longer drowning in guilt.

"You look mighty pretty today," I drawl, trying to be my best southern church boy.

Harper bats her eyelashes at me. "You don't clean up so bad yourself. I had no idea that football star Cain Kent owned a suit, or anything other than Haven Football gear."

I scoff, "You saw me at homecoming. I looked like a dreamboat."

"Humbleness is next to Godliness," she jokes, as we sidle up to the refreshments table.

I pour the lemonade and hand it to her, filling the cups one by one, I can't help but bend down and plant a kiss on her cheek. "Do you think your grandma is going to kick me in the nuts?"

Harper chuckles. "No, but she does have a shotgun. I'd definitely bring those flowers next time or you might be staring down the barrel of it."

I pretend to shiver with nerves. "So, you going to come to my game this Friday? Now that we're dating and all."

"Who says we're dating?" She tries to smile but I see the question in her eyes.

She wants me to define what this is.

And I want to be dating, after all of the bullshit that I've been weighing back and forth. "I do ... that is, if you want to be with me?"

After a second, Harper smiles, moving toward me even though she has lemonade cups in her hands. "I guess I could live with that. So where do I sit for this game?"

I sling my arm around her shoulder as we walk back to the table, both balancing cups of cold juice. "In the student section.

But you'll wear my jersey, so that everyone knows you're my girl."

"Ew, the jersey you sweated in? No thanks." She wrinkles her cute nose.

As we near the table where our respective families sits, I grin. "Don't worry, I'll wash it. But I want you wearing my number. I've never asked a girl to do that before ... it would mean a lot to me."

Harper looks up. "Then, I'll be there, in your jersey."

23

CAIN

R*aise the Cain! Raise the Cain! Raise the Cain!*

Even though we're playing in enemy territory, on another team's field, the chant for my touchdown rings out into the Friday night lights above.

My heart is pumping so fast that I can hear the blood whooshing in my ears. We've fought tooth and nail for this win, and in another forty-five seconds, we'll have pulled it out.

I'm sweating, even though the temperature has dropped to an unseasonably cool fifty degrees. Up in the stands, people are wrapped in blankets or sporting winter coats.

Standing on the sidelines, I should be watching our defense shut down the only offense still standing in the way of our trip to the state championship. But I'm not. Instead, my head is twisted back over my shoulder, looking for the one face in the crowd that I want to find.

A couple of bleacher rows up, standing next to Imogen, is my girl. Harper. My jersey is enormous on her small frame, more of a dress over her layers of long sleeves and sweatshirts than a shirt. She has one of those soft, furry-looking earmuff headbands pushing back her blond hair, and I can see that the tip of her nose is red.

My heart beats double-time, it's such a turn-on to see her standing there in my jersey. Like I belong to her, and she belongs to me.

I haven't really advertised that we're dating, although I'm sure the gossip mill of Haven High has assumed since we're always together. And I haven't told my friends that I'm dropping out of the competition. I'm still trying to figure out the best way to avoid a seismic eruption from anyone in my life ... meaning no one finds out anything that will hurt them.

We win the game as the cheers erupt from our section of the opposing team's stands, and after standing in a line to pat the backs of the losing players, I head for the locker room.

My post-game shower and dress is so quick that I'm pretty sure the tips of my wet hair will freeze when I go outside, but I want to catch Harper before she drives home. Not that I won't see her there in an hour, but I could use a post-game congratulatory kiss. Or seven.

As I head for the parking lot, I see our team bus, and someone standing right next to the folding doors makes me stop.

Annabelle Mills leans against the side of the school bus, her cheerleading uniform pristine.

"I see you have a new girlfriend. Thought you didn't do those, Cain. Oh wait, you just don't do relationships. You ruin them for other people." Anna's face contorts into an ugly sneer.

I had drunkenly taken Annabelle's virginity during a party in the fall of our sophomore year. It was something we both never should have done, but it was a tally mark for the competition.

For Annabelle, it meant ruining the relationship she was in, with a senior baseball player who kicked my ass at the time. And since then, she blamed me for ruining her and all of the heartbreak that followed. She felt like I owed her something, like another chance or another lay because I'd somehow fucked-up her life.

"What happened between us, Anna, it was a mistake. We both know that. But what you did to Boone, that is on you. I was single, you had some agenda with your boyfriend or whatever he was. You made that decision."

I was tired after the game, wanted to do nothing more than sit on this bus and text Harper, now that I couldn't even kiss her, and I didn't need Anna in my face right now. She and I had had this fight a dozen times over the years, and tonight, my victory night, was not going to be ruined by her queen bee shit.

"Don't talk to me about Boone. Ever," she snaps. "I'm telling you, that trailer trash girl is beneath you."

My blood heats with anger. "And I'm telling you, do not talk about Harper. Ever."

A sneaking smile lights her face. "Oh my God ... you like her? You actually like this ... this slut."

"Anna, I swear to God." My fists ball up, and while I'll never hit a woman, I may punch the brick building next to her cheek.

She hoots a laugh. "So instead of having sex with her, like your little competition rules lay out, you fell for her? This is too good. Cain Kent, I never thought I'd see the day. Serves you right, messing up my life like you did, now you're in love with a dirty peasant. Karma is a cold bitch."

I'm not even listening to her insulting Harper, because my mind is still stuck on the fact that she just referenced the competition. "How do you know about those rules?"

My mouth is dry and my breaths are coming out in puffs. Anna is going to bring this all toppling down on me. If Harper finds out just how much and how long I've been lying, she'll never forgive me. She'll never see me again.

Annabelle's grin is pure evil. "Oh, Cain, are you really that naïve? Everyone who is anyone in this school knows about that pissing contest between you and the boys. You're lucky we keep letting you do it, unencumbered. But ... I think little miss Florida Keys might deserve to know what the guy she considers her boyfriend is up to. His real motives. Because to you, she isn't your girlfriend, right? Or at least I haven't heard any chatter about you two making it official."

My veins sing with fury, my heart thumps with the guilt and yearning that mix when it comes to Harper. I should have told her from the jump, immediately when I knew I was developing feelings I should have come clean and bowed out of the competition. I care too much about her now, and don't want to lose her.

But with this hanging over my head, with Annabelle holding the axe that can chop it all down ... it's bound to come out.

"Don't worry, I'm not going to tell her, Cain. My allegiance is to you, after all. We're cut from the same cloth, unlike Harper. But I can't wait to see her face when she does find out."

Annabelle saunters away merrily, like she's just helped the homeless instead of killed a cat.

The bus ride home is a nightmare. Instead of celebrating that we made it to state, I'm jonesing. My leg is rattling like a drug addict, I'm jumpy and sweating, even though the game was over more than half an hour ago. My mind keeps racing through scenarios of Harper finding out, and they all end with my heart aching like it was sliced open.

As soon as we get back to the high school, I jump in my Jeep, hightailing it out of there to the shouts of my teammates, yelling about where we are going to party.

I could care less about that.

I drive straight to Harper's house, not caring what time it is. I pull to the end of the drive, and text her.

Cain: *Meet me in the fields by the woods.*

Harper: *Two minutes.*

She must be anxious to see me too.

I sneak through the property, careful to stay in the shadows of the trees at the edge of it, and fearful of Harper's words about her grandmother's shotgun.

True to her word, she comes running quietly at me from the fields, the house behind her back in the distance. She doesn't slow down as she approaches, and soon she's jumping into my arms, straddling me as I absorb her impact.

She crushes her lips down onto mine, and I thrust my hands into her hair, fiercely jutting my tongue against hers.

It's in this moment that I know I'm head over heels for this girl. Like a snap of fingers, the idea is tangible and real, it almost makes me drop to my knees with Harper in my arms.

And I know I have to protect this against anything that could tear us apart.

24

CAIN

I've fallen for her.

This was never supposed to happen. Harper was supposed to be a mark, a conquest. I'm so blinded by my feelings that I'm thinking about talking to my friends about love?

I have to stop this. Once I leave Haven, I'm leaving everyone in it behind as well. I have dreams, goals. There are so many things I need to focus on, besides Harper Posy, to get me to where I want to go.

That all-too-familiar urge starts bubbling inside my chest. Poisoning the feelings that have built so rapidly for a girl I only met two months ago. Only one of my friends has ever seriously become involved with a girl, and he's the only one that I trust to give me advice. And not go blabbing to our other friends that I might be in love.

Will sits at a desk in the library, the world around him gone as books are piled up surrounding him. To be honest, Will is not your typical football player, and yet, he's just always been part of the friend group. He's nerdy, has a serious girlfriend, likes to get good grades, doesn't have an ultimate dream of getting to the big time.

"Bud," I say in greeting, and sit down in the chair across the table from him.

Will looks up, nodding. "Kent, what's up?"

He's in the middle of studying, and I can see that I interrupted him, so I go for the jugular. "I think I might be in love."

I swear, Will almost snaps his pencil in half he's so surprised. "Um ... excuse me?"

I can feel a blush creep over my cheeks, and I hide my eyes under the visor of my hand. "The girl I'm seeing, how do I know if she's the real deal? I've never ..."

My voice trails off and I can see Will's mouth turn up in a smile. He's smug, the bastard. "You've never felt anything for a girl other than the stir of your dick?"

"Something like that," I grumble.

Will taps his finger to his chin. "Well, do you want to see her all the time?"

I thought of Harper's pixie face. "Yeah."

"And when your with her, does your heart feel ... like it's melting?"

"Yes," I admit in a hushed tone.

"Holy shit, I never thought I'd see the day. Hell must have frozen over." Will's shit-eating grin makes me ball up a piece of notebook paper and throw it at him.

"Don't gloat, you prick. Tell me what I should do. Harper thinks I'm this good guy, and there is the competition, and my reputation ..." It overwhelms me.

Will frowns. "Loving this girl means you're going to have to forget about what other people think. Because when you're in love, you'd rather make that person happy over anything you'd want yourself. As for the competition ... I think you have to tell her and take that risk man. Better than her finding out from someone else. I told my girl when it came down to it ... not that I had the reputation that you did before we started dating."

"Thanks for that, man." I scowl at him.

I digest Will's words. Putting her before me, before anyone else. That was what love was? No wonder I'd never fallen in love with a woman, I had no idea what that felt like to receive from a person of the female gender. As for the competition, I just didn't know. It was a huge risk, both telling her and not telling her. It has been gnawing at me ever since I sat in that church, two pews away from her under the eye of God.

"For what it's worth ... I knew you had it in you." Will gives me a solemn nod. "And Harper, she seems like a good girl. Just don't screw this up, bro. I think she's going to be the one to tame you after all."

Screw it up. That was exactly what I was trying *not* to do.

That night, I once again find myself on the Posy property. But this time, I'm not skulking around the woods.

I brought some flowers, and a box of cookies from the cafe in town, and while Harper's mom had been smitten, her grandmother had scowled at me. At least she still let me sit at the dinner table.

I'd been a good boy throughout the meal, saying please and thank you, not cursing, had been extremely involved in conversation. It was safe to say that I was on my way to charming all three of the Posy women, Blanche had even smiled at me over the apple cobbler we'd eaten for dessert.

We talked about Harper's childhood obsession with Nancy Drew and the Boxcar children, her love of stray cats, and the right way to eat ice cream. I told them about accidentally ruining my dad's pair of army boots when he'd been home on leave when I was ten after I'd walked in newly-poured cement, and they'd laughed their heads off.

After, as the two older women shooed us out of the kitchen so they could clean up, Harper asked if I wanted to go for a walk as the sun set.

I hold her hand, loving the warmth of it. Will's words echoed in my head ... you know you're in love when you'd rather make that person happy than yourself.

"Were you just trying to get me out here to take advantage of me? Or because you knew I was shaking and terrified of your grandmother?" I squeeze her hand as we walk together.

"A little bit of both," she admits, laughing.

I'm gazing at the side of her baby blues, when I veer us right, out over the acres and acres of property.

"I thought you might want a tour of your land. You know, by the man, the myth and the legend himself." I point to myself.

"You know, it's a shame you're not more secure with yourself. And this is my family's land, if you forgot." Harper's sarcasm bleeds into her smirk.

"Yeah, but I've lived here longer, snuck onto it a number of times."

"I oughta tell my grandma that, she'll cook you like a pig with an apple in your mouth." Harper chuckles.

"I'd rather have something else in my mouth." I turn toward her, a funny but creepy smile on my face.

"You look like a gross hornball." Harper giggles.

"That's because I am." I tickle her; our path has taken us to one of the fields probably a mile out from the house.

There is nothing around but us, the setting sun, and the grass. The Texas air hums around us as the temperature starts to drop. She turns into my arms and my fingers skate on her ribs slow, turning into more of a caress than a tickle.

Slowly, I lower us into the grass, the blades of it tickling my skin and poking through the material of my sweatshirt. Harper is beneath me, her long blond hair splayed over the earth. I look down on her as glints of sunlight fall over her high cheekbones, and kiss them, first the right side and then the left.

Her hands wrap around my neck in a sigh, tying at the back, making her a part of me. "Cain ..."

That sweet voice in my ear, raspy and needy. I press myself, through my jeans, against her center and feel her squirm. I want to be inside of her so bad, I can feel the poison of my release backing up in my veins. But it's out of my hands; I won't push her to that step until she explicitly asks for it.

My hands fumble for the hem of her sweater, and I am surprised to see them shaking. I kiss her, as much to taste her as it is to get out of my own head, and then continue the search for skin with my hands.

Up, up, up they go, my fingers skimming under her shirt over her belly button. They smooth over the flat plane of her stomach and caress her ribs, and then I push the cups of her bra out of the way so that I can circle one perfect nipple.

"I want to see you," I breathe against her lips.

Harper sits up on her elbows and slips the sweater over her head, never losing eye contact with me. Then, she pushes me off of her, settling finally so that we're lying side by side. Her bra is a peach color, so delicate against her skin. My hands go to both exquisitely rounded peaks, rolling her nipples between my thumb and forefingers.

She cries out and arches into me, her hands landing on the zipper of my jeans. I freeze, knowing we haven't come this far yet. Knowing she has *never* come this far.

"You don't have to," I choke. Because I *so* want her to.

"What if I want to?" Harper smiles, but the confident look

she's trying to portray is given away by the nervous glaze in her baby blues.

Her hands shake even more than mine had as she unbuckles my pants and pulls the zipper down. To distract her a little, I imitate her motions on her pants, drawing them down around her hips. My hand dives into her underwear, and bypasses her clit as I plunge one long finger inside of her.

"Oh gosh ..." she breathes, her own fingers teetering on the waistband of my boxers.

I finger her, pressing on the spot inside of her until she releases those breathy little moans, while her hand ventures into my underwear and down. I cant my hips, I can't help it, trying to guide her toward my aching shaft.

After what feels like a lifetime of Harper exploring the skin south of my waist, her small hand wraps around my cock, the little pressure she's applying feeling like goddamn water in the middle of the desert.

"Shit ..." I hiss out as Harper pulls up, an experimental tug.

"Is this .., okay?" The unsureness vibrates in her throat.

"If you stop, I'll die." I smile tightly at her, trying to coax her to keep going.

We're pleasuring each other in tandem, my finger sinking into her as she holds tight to my cock, stroking me up and down. Each time her thumb hits the blunt head of me, I suck in a breath, sparks of electricity shooting down my spine and directly into my balls.

Harper is whimpering now, and I don't know if she realizes she's doing it. We're making out, our kisses sloppy and heated, as our hands bring the other to the edge.

"Cain ... Oh my ... Cain, I think ..." Her breaths are labored and her hips are grinding down so hard on my hand that I almost can't keep it steady inside of her.

I press that spot again, rubbing her clit with the heel of my palm. This makes her gasp, and I repeat the motion, which only makes her start stroking me faster. At the base of my spine, I can feel my climax start. Gripping my balls, shooting from my head to my toes, leaving tingles in its wake.

My hand moves against Harper one more time, and a louder moan than I've ever heard her make comes careening from her throat. At the same time, her whole fist shoots up, brushing the sensitive underside of my dick and causing a chain reaction inside me. I suck in a breath as I feel the come explode from my tip, coating her hand. I look into her eyes as the ecstasy washes over my flesh, and see that the same bliss is stealing over her features.

In this moment, I know that I love her. And I have to bite down on my tongue to keep those words from slipping out of my mouth.

25

HARPER

It had only happened last night, and yet, my mind, body and heart still burn with my first orgasm.

Now I understand. I get it, comprehend why lusting after another's body had started wars and committed men and women alike to insanity.

Lying on the couch, watching a *Friends* rerun, my hand glides across my stomach and moves lower, to the path Cain had blazed less than twenty-four hours ago in the fields. I can still feel the imprint of his fingers there, the way they scorched me. And on my fingers ... I can still feel him. The soft steel, the warmth of his flesh in my palm, the way I made him growl and convulse under my touch.

I'd felt powerful. I'd felt like I could bring Cain to his knees. It had been such an ego-boost, even if I had had to wipe my hand off in the grass. That part was a little embarrassing for me, but Cain had not seemed to mind. He'd kissed me with the intensity of a thousand suns afterward, and I'd been reassured that for my first time giving a hand job, I'd done a pretty good job.

Third base. I'd gotten to third base with a boy. And one that I really, really like. One that I may even be in love with. But far be it from me to ever say those words out loud.

Yes, it is true that Cain and I are dating. But telling someone that they were the only guy you'd ever felt your heart thump double-time over was a different beast all in itself. And he's Cain Kent, for God's sakes. Sometimes, I still wonder what he sees in me.

The front door to Grandma's ranch opens just as Mom comes skipping into the open concept front hallway slash living room to greet the people walking through it.

"Michael, so glad you guys could come for dinner." She kisses her boyfriend on the cheek and he smiles at her.

What the hell? Who was "you guys"?

I got my answer as soon as I round the corner, to see my mom's boyfriend of a month and his daughter, the queen bee and my worst nightmare, standing in the tiny foyer.

"Mom, what are they doing here?" I jump up in surprise, trying to secretly check my teeth and smell my armpits.

Thank God I have jeans and a semi-nice shirt on, still in them from school, because it would have been totally uncool to have greeted Annabelle Mills in my Justin Bieber T-shirt I'd gotten in fourth grade.

"Don't worry, I was brought here against my will," Annabelle practically snarled at me.

Mom and Michael have been hot and heavy for a month now. And I do mean that because the first time I met him, I'd caught them in his car making out with the windows fogged. Besides that awkward encounter, though, I like him. He is a nice guy, has a good job, treats my mother like a princess, and seems to be a good dad. Even though his child is the spawn of Satan. But he couldn't help that, I reasoned.

"I invited them for dinner." My mother smiles at me, but her eyes hold that look that told me I better be nice or she'd beat me with a spoon, Grandma-style, later.

Biting my own tongue, so that I couldn't protest, I simply follow as she takes everyone to the kitchen. I should have been suspicious when I'd smelled the scent of meatloaf wafting through the house; It was Mom's best recipe and I should have guessed that she was making it for company.

But how I was going to make it through a dinner with Annabelle is beyond me. I don't even have Grandma here as a buffer because tonight is her weekly bridge game.

Annabelle has mostly left me alone since I had become Cain's girlfriend, but I still saw her snickering to her posse and pointing at me in the cafeteria. I knew she didn't like me, and now that my mother was about to try to bond with her, I knew she'd like me even less.

"Harper, fill the water glasses, please," Mom instructs me.

I help her set the table as she lays the food out, while Michael and Annabelle sit there.

"I wish you'd let me help, sweetie." Michael kisses her arm as she sets a bowl of corn down.

"Nonsense! I'm cooking for you, you're my guest. Enjoy it." She winks at him.

I want to vomit.

"You're such a good server, Harper. Is that training from a waitress job?" Annabelle sneers, and I know her compliment is supposed to be backhanded.

Mom didn't pick up on this. "Oh no, Harper works at a bait and tackle shop. She did when we lived in Florida, too. How about you, Annabelle? Do you have a job, honey?"

My mom is trying to get to know the daughter of her boyfriend. What I should have mentioned is that this girl's bite is worse than her bark. And her bark is damn mean.

"Oh, I don't work. I'm way too busy with cheer." She smiles, talking to my Mom like she's a five-year-old who just wouldn't understand.

"Yeah, but that'll be ending soon. I think it's about time you worked, made some money instead of spending mine," Michael ribs her.

Annabelle shoots a death glare my way as if I am the one responsible for her having to get a job.

Once we all sit down and started eating, you could cut the tension in the air with a knife.

"How was your week at school, honey?" Michael asks Mom.

She smiles, cutting into her meatloaf and swiping it in ketchup. "Oh, it was good. My class is great this year, the kids are just so much more attentive than my old school, which is nice. We had a little history lesson about Native American life in America to prepare for Thanksgiving."

I smile at my mom. She is so good at what she does, the perfect teacher to mold young minds. And I was happy that her students here were better than the ones in our old hometown.

I speak up, choosing to make the best out of this, even if I can feel Annabelle's scowl on me the entire time. "Every year, Mom and I churn a small pot of butter, just like the settlers used to do. It takes so long, but it really is amazing how delicious the real thing is."

This was one of my favorite traditions, one started from my history buff mother.

Michael chuckles. "That sounds like a real arm workout, but I'd sure love to try that. I remember growing up, my dad would bring us to this tiny farm stand off the interstate that made their own cheese from start to finish. God, I dream about that cheese sometimes still."

"I spend Thanksgiving with my mother," Annabelle speaks up, directing that little tidbit at my own mom.

But, ever the optimist, my mother smiles at her. "That's lovely. Do y'all have any traditions you like?"

Annabelle frowns, annoyed that she hasn't upset her. "We don't really."

Mom hasn't really told me a lot about Michael's divorce or his ex-wife, but I have a feeling that Annabelle lives full time with him for a reason.

"Well, maybe if you wanted to do something around the holiday with us, we could make a new tradition." Mom smiles, and Michael clasps her hand from across the small kitchen table.

"Yeah, not likely," Annabelle says under her breath with the intention for all of us to hear it.

"That's enough," Michael says sharply. "We are together now, and I know you might want to act like a brat about it, but we're going to be spending a lot of time with Clara and Harper. So get used to it. I'm not saying we have to be a family, but we need to be nice to each other. To get along."

I would not want to disappoint this man, that's for sure. He's not scary, but he is a genuine, honest person, and I have a feeling that letting him down makes you feel like crap.

"Yes, Daddy." Annabelle hangs her head, and I think that I see real remorse in her eyes.

The rest of our dinner goes along somewhat peacefully, and I hope, for my mother's sake, that Annabelle's attitude toward me changes. We don't have to even be friends, but a détente would be nice.

26

HARPER

Cain has ignored me all day. Stalking away from me before the bell for homeroom, after not even meeting me at my locker.

Was this it? Had he broken up with me? Not that we'd even had the boyfriend-girlfriend talk ... but we'd been making out and going to parties together and holding hands after school and that was more than I'd done with any other boy in my life. He'd even called me his girl.

My chest had hung heavy with emotion all day. The sense of dread, the feeling of not knowing, the curse of impending heartbreak. I knew he would do this to me, and I'd been stupid enough to be swept away in the golden boy pursing me.

I was an idiot. And now, on top of being an idiot, I was going to cry over a guy who could care less than to even have a conversation ending things.

Cain is in the parking lot at the end of the day as I walk by, plugging my headphones into my ears and getting ready for a litany of sad country breakup songs.

"Looking sexy." He winks at me as I pass, that long, muscled frame leaning against the hood of his Jeep.

I should roll my eyes. I should keep walking. I should ignore the nagging embarrassment in my chest, that this guy can just so easily discard me. My mouth should stay shut.

But I just can't help it. Cain Kent is a womanizer, and he needs to be taught a lesson.

I round on him. "You know what? You're a scared, sorry excuse of a man. Because you're not even man enough to tell me we're done. Who does that? You're not so above everyone in this town that you can just treat the rest of us like dirt under your shoes. Or excuse me, football cleats, because Lord knows that if you wear those around these parts, you consider yourself a god."

My face is heated and I'm panting by the time I finish my short diatribe, and I want to peel the navy blue cardigan I wore today off my shoulders. It's sticking to me, suffocating me.

Cain's green eyes are slits, and I can tell he's pissed. Grady is parked next to his car, and he can hear us. So can a gaggle of students procrastinating going home, having conversations in the parking lot.

"Why should I have to tell you we're done when I didn't even say that anything was started?"

Oh, fuck this. "You're a piece of shit."

I stomp up and wave my middle finger so close to his face that he could bite it if he wanted to. And then I stalk off, every muscle in my body singing with anger at how tight I'm tensing them.

I'm not sure how far I walk, or how many tears I let escape, but a horn sound breaks through Taylor Swift's "Teardrops on my Guitar" about ten minutes later. I'm halfway home, walking down the shoulder of one of the many farm roads in Haven, and I turn. I see Cain driving slowly next to me, his truck matching my pace.

Ignoring him, I keep walking. He speeds up, he's talking out of the open side of his truck where the driver's door should be, and I wrench my neck the other way so I don't have to look at him.

A minute later, he's parked, hopped out and is standing in front of me. Blocking my path.

His big, warm hands go to my shoulders, and I brush him off. Pulling an earbud out, I hiss through my teeth, "Leave me alone."

"I'm sorry, okay?" Those pools, the colors of freshly-mowed grass, won't look at my face.

"Psh, yeah, you sound really apologetic. You're an asshole, Cain. You can't even admit that what we're doing is—"

I'm about to say dating, which will dig me even deeper into the heartbreak hole, when he interrupts me.

"I'm having a shitty day, okay?"

Cain's entire tone changes, and a somber look steals over his face. I'm still enraged and feel like my heart is split in two, but I can't help asking what's wrong. He never admits to feeling a thing ... this is a first.

"What's going on?"

His shoulders shrug and his arms hang limply by his side. For a guy who always look like Hercules ... right now, he looks defeated.

"I haven't heard from my dad in four days. That's never happened before." I can see the pain radiating from his eyes.

He doesn't have to say that he thinks his father might be injured ... or worse. We all know what goes on in war zones.

Immediately, my malice toward him evaporates. I reach a hand out, place it on his bicep. "Maybe he's just in a remote part of wherever he is. Maybe he isn't allowed to reach out right now."

Cain steps into my embrace, surprising me. "Or maybe he's dead." His assumption is muffled.

"Don't think like that." I hug him to me, in the middle of the dirt shoulder of this road.

We stand like this, intertwined, as he breathes me in. My heart sews itself back together at the sight where it started to tear just an hour ago. He wasn't ignoring me, he was trying to shut out the world.

"Sometimes, when I miss my dad more than I usually do, I watch *A Few Good Men*," I confess, stroking my hands up and down his strong, toned back.

Through his T-shirt, I feel him tense and then shiver. His hands move up the column of my body, and around the back of my neck where he cups it, moving so that he can look into my eyes. "Why that movie?"

It's like we're soothing each other with touch ... it doesn't much matter what the conversation is about. Right here, on a road where anyone could see us, we're practically fore-playing.

"My mom told me it was his favorite. Loved the cast, loved the plot ... he almost went into the military because of it but then decided to be a firefighter instead." I reach up, brushing my hands through his dark mop of hair.

Cain presses his lips to mine, not kissing but speaking into them. "I'd be an orphan if I lost him. What would I even do?"

And I can see, that this is his greatest fear. As someone who has had it happen, losing a father, I know how tragic it can be.

"It's a horrible thing, and you never recover. But the pain gets easier ... even for me who doesn't even remember how to picture my dad's face. And you celebrate him in little ways, like watching his favorite movie or keeping a picture of him on your bedside table."

"I am sorry, babe." He holds me tight to him. "Can you come over?"

This will be a new step, another level to our relationship. I haven't been over to Cain's house yet, and have come to regard it as his sanctuary. Now, he's inviting me in.

I nod, and we climb into his truck.

Four hours later, after we made a dinner of frozen pizza and green beans—the vegetables had been at my insistence because who knows the last time this eighteen-year-old boy who lived alone had eaten anything healthy—we sit on the floor of Cain's room, looking at his grade school yearbooks.

"Oh my gosh, look at MK." I point to her first grade picture on the page and giggle. "She was so cute."

"Hey, I was cute too!" Cain's voice holds offense.

I stare at the photo of the little boy in a row of pictures. He's got shaggy black hair, is missing a front tooth, and those green eyes gleam with a smile.

"Yes, you were adorable." I sit up on my knees and plant a kiss on his cheek.

Tonight, I've learned so much more about Cain Kent. I perused his bookshelves. Okay, so maybe I pored over them, gathering insights about his interests by the titles on the spines. He'd read me some of his favorite passages, something so romantic that I'd nearly fainted. He also walked me through the house, reliving different memories as we walked past. The bottom step on the stairs that he chipped his front tooth on while trying to do the worm down the hallway in sixth grade. The wood-burning stove in the kitchen that had originally sat in his grandparents' house forty years ago.

My heart had fallen harder with each step through the canvas of Cain's life.

He yawns, stretching, and looks at the clock. "It's getting late. Let's go to bed."

Instantly, my palms start to sweat. "Cain ..."

He smooths a lock of my hair. "Not like that, Harper. You should know by now that I'm not going to push you for that. You have to tell me if and when you want to have sex. But tonight, I just want to sleep with you. As in, lie in the same bed together, feel you against me all night."

My heart fluttered. "But, what will I tell my mom?"

He smirks. "You've never snuck out or told her you'd be somewhere you weren't, huh?"

I blush. "I told you I wasn't that much of a social butterfly in Florida."

"Tell her you're sleeping over MK's. She'll cover for us." His eyes hypnotize me until I had the courage to lie.

After my phone call to Mom, which was uneventful and she questioned me about nothing, I texted MK and she said of course she'd cover. And then added a wink face and sixteen exclamation points.

I walk back into Cain's bedroom, and he is already in bed, shirtless. I can't see what is going on underneath the sheets, but I hope to God there are boxers or shorts because I already know I'm not going to be able to get any shut eye with his body next to mine.

"Get in here." He grins at me.

God, he's sexy. "What ... I didn't bring anything to wear."

"I left you a shirt there." He points to the folded tee at the edge of the bed.

Picking it up, I look around. While he's seen me naked, I feel totally self-conscious changing right in front of him. "I'm just going to ..."

"You can change in the bathroom, babe." He nods, understanding.

After I change into his T-shirt, that comes down to my knees and smells just like Cain, I crawl into bed with him.

"Mm, your hair smells amazing." Cain scoops me up, pulling me into him.

We're entwined, our legs tangling as my arms go to his bare

chest and his wrap around me. My core is slick, but my heart also soars. This isn't about lust; not tonight. Cain needs comfort, and the sentiment in the air is one of compassion and coziness.

"This is perfect. All I needed was your cuddles." He buries his head in my hair, while my face burrows into his shoulder.

"Good night, Cain." I don't know what else to say, because I don't want to break the spell between us.

That night, we sleep in each other's arms. Touching, not in an erotic way, but just an exploration of the other's body. It's the most intimate thing I've ever done with another person.

With every passing minute, I feel each piece of my heart turn against me, and mark itself as Cain's. In the middle of the night, while he breathes softly, I stare at his gorgeous face.

And realize that I'm in love with him.

27

HARPER

I've had too much to drink.

The world starts spinning and I look at the red Solo cup in my hand, knowing that I've lost count. What is this, four, five? My mouth tastes like acidic beer, and the ground won't seem to stay in once place.

I felt more relaxed at this weekend's party, knowing more people and on the arm of Cain. He is the golden boy, and I am his girl. So I participated in the merriment, in the flip cup game and the dancing as the country music floated over my head. I lost track of said boyfriend, well, I wasn't sure how long ago. Mary-Kate had dared me to do a funnel and so I'd done one. And then another.

It wasn't like I'd never drank before. My first beer had been at the age of twelve when one of the older boys in the trailer park had offered me one from his six-pack. That was the way of life around there.

But I wanted to celebrate. I'd written "the end" on my novel, and now I just had to market and publish it. Almost two years' worth of my life, and I'd completed it. I felt on top of the world.

But, I'd never been this wasted before. My stomach feels like it might upend itself at any moment.

And then I bump into the one person I should avoid at all costs. "Ugh, stop grinding on me, you bitch."

I turn to see Annabelle, her perfect brown waves still intact on the humid night. Normally, I'd shrink away, not wanting the confrontation.

But the beer fuels my inhibitions. "Oh, look, if it isn't the queen bee herself! Everyone, let's bow at her feet."

Annabelle looks like I've slapped her. "You should, trailer trash."

"Well, looks like your father lies down with trailer trash then! Because he sure does love my mother." I'm being petty and childish, but I can't stop.

"Yeah, well, I already know what it's like to lie down with that man of yours. Or wait, is he my man, then? I guess you got my sloppy seconds." For the second time at a party I'd been to in this town, Annabelle Mills has brought my tower crumbling down.

I'm wobbling on my feet, searching for Cain through the bodies before Annabelle even finished her sentence. When I finally find him, standing in front of the fire talking to Grady, I stomp up.

"You fucked Annabelle?!" I was hysterical, a drunk slob. But I couldn't help myself.

Cain turns, staring at me, as others turn to watch. "Babe, why don't we go somewhere—"

I cut him off. "No! Tell me! Did you have sex with her?" I stomp my foot like a child.

My boyfriend takes my hand and leads me across the party, out into the woods and to the field where he parked his truck. Once we're there, I tug my arm from his.

"You are an asshole!" Some of the spit from my mouth lands on his face in my fit of anger.

"And you're drunk. And unreasonable. You need to calm down." He touches my shoulder.

"Don't." I shrug him off. "Did you or did you not sleep with her?"

The long grass whispers in the wind as Cain sighs. Noises from the party in the distance haunt us, the laughter and music fluttering through our argument.

"I did. Sophomore year, two years before I ever met you. Before I even knew you existed. And we weren't a thing, it was a mistake. I never should have done it, and now it's coming back to bite me in the ass because you're drunk and you and Annabelle are having a catfight."

Cain is pissed off, and I realize he was never going to tell me. "You were never going to tell me, were you?"

I'm being unreasonable, he's right. It happened years ago, before we'd ever known each other, or known about each other.

Cain throws his hands up, turning away from me and then back again. "No, I probably wasn't! It meant nothing. You're the only thing that matters to me, the only girl who has ever meant a thing. I fucking love you, Harper. Isn't that enough?"

I blink. "You love me?"

He looks shocked, like he hadn't really meant to blurt that out. Ducking his head, he kicks a boot against the dirt. "Well ... yeah. I do."

I go to him, still swaying, but a smile has broken out on my face. Tipping his chin up to meet my eyes, I caress his cheek. "I love you, too."

A grin blossoms on his lips, his green eyes searching mine. Sweetly, he places a kiss on my lips, and then breathes against them. "Great, now can we forget this stupid thing? You're the one

I love. And we're supposed to be celebrating you. I'm so proud that you finished writing your book. Let's focus on that, please?"

I could listen to him say those four little letters for a thousand years. "Yes."

We walk back to the party hand in hand, a couple of people looking at us but then ultimately forgetting we'd left in a fit of yelling. As if finishing my book wasn't grand enough, I was on cloud nine after Cain's admission.

I stick to water for the next hour, my head clearing a bit, as Cain plays game after game of beer pong, never losing. I guess the quarterback had a rep to protect.

Going to the cooler for another water, I feel a hand grab and squeeze my ass. I turn swiftly. "What the heck?"

Josiah, one of the guys that Cain plays football with, is standing there, a leering smirk on his face. "Hey, baby, nice ass."

"Um ..." I freeze, not knowing how to respond. It's clear he is drunk, but ...

"I heard you and Kent fighting before. You know you could lean on my shoulder if you want. Or ride my saddle." He winks, groping my hip as I stand there.

When I hear the word saddle, I push him away. "Stop it. I'm with Cain."

"Psh, boy just wants you to ride his junk. I can show you a better time, new girl. Hop on." He thrust his hips at me, and I cringe, trying to back away.

But the cooler hits me behind the knees and I stumble.

And the next thing I know, I'm sitting on top of the thing, and Josiah is on the ground, moaning in pain.

"Don't ever touch her again, fucker." Cain is pointing down at him, his face an angry shade of red.

"I was just messing around ..." Josiah groaned.

"By touching her when she told you to go away? You're a real prick, Josiah."

Cain moves to me, ignoring the asshole writhing on the ground. "You okay, baby?"

I nod, trying to steady my shaky heart and breath. "Yeah, just … shaken up. He didn't do anything though, not really."

He kisses the side of my forehead as he pulls me against him, as if he could have just lost me. "No, he did do something. That's harassment, or haven't you been watching the news. Any guy who touches you without your consent is wrong."

Surprise blooms in my chest. "I had no idea you were a proponent for the Me Too movement."

"I might be an asshole, but I'm not an abuser." He chuckles into my hair.

By now, Josiah has slunk off, and I unwind Cain's hands from around me and lace them through mine. But before I tell him that I want to go home, he winces.

"What's wrong?"

He holds his hand up between us. His right one. The golden hand, the one that will take him places. His pointer finger is bent sideways, and one of his knuckles is bleeding.

"Oh my God, Cain. Your hand." I breathe, panicking.

He starts to walk away from the bonfire, out toward his car again. "Shh, come here."

I follow him, his long strides too fast for me to keep up.

"You have to pop it back in for me." Cain holds his hand out to me when we reach his Jeep again.

My heart quickens. "Um, no. No … I can't."

Cain stares at me. "Babe, just pop it back in. No one else can know about this."

I'm scared by the fear in his tone. Cain Kent doesn't get scared, but right now, his face would say otherwise. I take a deep breath, reaching out with shaking hands, and try to resolve the rapid beating of my heart in my ears. Taking his right hand in my own two, I touch a finger to his crooked digit. And without thinking, I grab it suddenly, pulling it straight like one would a fishing rod you wanted to reel in.

My boyfriend lets out a yelp, hopping away from me as he clutches his hand to him. "Fuck, fuck, fuck …"

I stand there, the buzz leaking out of me, sobered from the injury to his hand. I want to go to him, tell him I'm sorry that he had to defend me, that it was my fault he had hurt himself.

"Baby?" My voice sounds so unsure.

Cain straightens, walking to me, a small smile on his face. "It's fine. Let me take you home."

But I knew that it wasn't fine.

28

CAIN

What Harper and I have is the kind of love singers croon about in country songs. It's the love that every director of a romantic movie hopes will translate to viewers. It's the kind of love that novels are written about, that authors painstakingly try to capture in their words.

It's a heated, Texas love. One that runs wild through the fields and buzzes with the honey bees in the late afternoon sun. It burns through my heart and leaves me thirsty for her every second of the day.

I thought a love like this was bullshit. That it didn't exist and those who said it did were just hopeless suckers. But I'd been wrong.

Not until this feeling of incompletion, because she isn't within an inch of you, steals over your limbs and joints and blood, do you understand a love like this.

We're now the couple every one secretly hates. I steal kisses before I drop her off at every class, and she wears my jersey to school on game days.

I can't believe that once, I tried to push her away. Tried to ignore her and make her feel worthless. And Harper had come to me all the same, knocking down my defenses and working her way in so that I would accept her comfort.

That bad part is, I wanted her to. I wanted her to not put up with my whining, with my treatment of her. I wanted her attention and kindness. And after she'd slept in my bed, after I'd held her all night, I knew that there was no untangling her from the way she'd wound around my heart.

She was embedded, and I was completely giving over to it. It wouldn't be easy, and although I hadn't even talked any of this through with her, I knew we'd make it work. I'd never wanted someone so bad in my entire life ... and I was anything but a quitter. I was going to work as hard at this relationship as I did at football. Was going to give it two hundred percent.

Which is what I was giving to football right now. The locker room shakes with the cheers of the crowds above, the huge stadium at a nearby college was the neutral site for tonight's state championship. Somewhere up there, Harper sat with my grandfather and her mom, grandma and Michael Mills. My knees shook, not with nerves, but with the anxiousness of wanting to get out onto that field.

But, there is a tinge of sadness that my dad couldn't be here for this. I'd finally gotten in touch with him; he'd been on a covert mission that he hadn't been able to tell me about until it was over. He was perfectly fine, safe and in one piece, and he'd been stoked to hear that we'd made state.

Once the locker room had mostly cleared out, with most of the players meeting in the conference room in this swanky facility to pump each other up, I addressed my finger. It ached and hurt each time I touched it, but I hadn't told a soul except for Harper. I wasn't letting one fucking finger ruin the rest of my life.

I'd downed six Advil, put a numbing cream on it, and was going to tape it to high heaven and then claim I liked to tape my wrist and hand for big games. I'd play it off as a superstition instead of an injury, and pray nobody questioned me. We were going to win this game, and I was going to throw that ball even if it meant pain radiated through my arm with each launch.

I joined my brothers, my teammates, as Coach walked in to give us his speech.

"Tonight is not about winning or losing. Tonight is about leaving your mark on this game, for this school, in your state, forever. For you seniors, this is your last game together as the band of brothers you've created over these last four years. Go out there and play like you've trained. Be better than you ever have before. Be invincible. Be gods."

We all look at him, his wisdom golden fuel pumping through our veins.

Everyone turns to me, and I nod. "Hands in. Haven on three. One, two, three—"

"HAVEN!" The word rings out, and then we're running, sprinting while the adrenaline pumps through the group like a drug.

We break out onto the field, cleats slapping against turf, the first of the players breaking through the banner that the cheerleaders are holding up. Immediately, I turn on the part of my brain that banishes everything out but the game.

The pain, the noise, the fans, the pressure ... I push it all out until the only thing I can see is that football in my hand after we win the coin toss and decide to receive on the first kickoff.

As soon as I get the first play in my helmet radioed from Coach, I bring my boys together, rifling off instructions like a drill sergeant.

I'm not usually such a stickler, but I want this game to play out with surgical-like precision. My hand is throbbing underneath the tape, and every time the ball is hiked into my hands, I have to bite the inside of my cheek from crying out in pain.

But I grin and bear it. I throw pass after pass, the tingling sensation of painful pins and needles moving up my arm as the quarters tick down on the scoreboard.

I tune it all out. The crowd. My team. The coaches' voices. The defensive plays that happen when I'm on the sidelines.

The only things I think about are myself, my arm, the ball, and spotting my retrievers or running backs. If I run myself like a machine, let the years of training and drills take over my body, then I will carry us to a win.

If I bring us a victory, I'll have unlocked my future.

"Are you sure you don't want to celebrate with your teammates? I feel bad." Harper turns her face to me, the moonlight illuminating her iridescent blue eyes.

"I told you, the only person I want to celebrate with is you." I wrap my arms tighter around her.

We're lying on top of a blanket on the banks of Lake McCray, my favorite spot out here. The fact that I've brought Harper to my spot, the one I usually only drive out to alone, is a big step.

You would think that telling each other we loved each other would be the biggest step of all, well, of course besides sex. But there was something about showing another person the quiet, dark places of yourself. Harper had seen my fear over the absence of my dad, and I had seen the sorrow inside of her from losing her's at such a young age. I'd invited her to my house, to sleep in my bed ... which were two things I'd never done with a girl before.

And now we were here. Lying entwined on the shores of my favorite spot, celebrating our win at state. I'd taken off after the bus dropped us back at Haven High, kissing Gramps and saying hi to Blanche and Clara before taking Harper by the hand and hurriedly jumping in my Jeep. My teammates had been shouting about parties and The Atrium, but all I wanted to do was be alone with the girl I love.

All I wanted to do was bask in the quiet glory of this night, to look at the open Texas sky and just be Cain Kent, high school football legend, for one more night. Because after the clock struck twelve, I was property of the media, the college system, and the scouts all over the country who would be tracking my progress until I decided to declare for the draft. But right now, I could lie on this blanket under the stars in my hometown with the most beautiful girl I know. Right now, I could be a human kid for just a little while longer.

"I'm so proud of you." Harper lifts my injured hand, kisses the tender skin and bones there.

I try not to wince as she does it. "Knowing you were up in those stands made me want to perform harder. I think you need to come to college with me. You're my good luck charm."

Her eyes go wide as saucers. We haven't talked about what will happen after graduation … at least not yet. It's still months away, and I haven't wanted to burst our bubble. But now that I've said it, I don't want to take the words back. I want her to come with me. I want to spend all my time with her.

"I'm not sure I want to go to college. But I do know that I want to be with you," she says quietly, a muffled thought into my neck.

I don't feel like talking about such big things on a night like this, where I feel invincible. So I bridge the gap between us, sliding my tongue into her mouth. Harper melts into my lips, her sigh has become the most erotic song to me.

Quickly, things escalate. Her hands are pulling at the hem of my T-shirt, my fingers are slipping the jersey over her head and unfastening her bra. Both sets of pants come off, and suddenly, we're naked down to just my boxers that Harper is trying to slide over my hips.

I break off the kiss, hovering over her slim body as my breath comes out in hard gasps. "Let's slow down."

"I don't want to slow down." Harper pushes the last shred of clothing between us away and takes me in her hand.

Stars erupt in the corners of my eyes, and I have to stiffen every muscle in my body not to give in to the sensation she's bewitching me with.

"Baby … we don't have to do this tonight. I know you want to wait."

"But I love you. I'm ready and I'm in love." She pants underneath me.

"And I love you enough to wait. I love you so much, Harper. And I want you to be sure about this. I don't want to pressure you."

Looking up, I see that she's biting her lip. The indecision is clear in her eyes. I make it for her.

"Let me love you in another way. I promise it will feel just as good."

Before she can answer, I slide down her body, kissing each inch of creamy, soft flesh as I go. I start at her knees, leaving airy pecks along the inseam of her legs. She's writhing beneath my exploration, and moaning so loud that she's going to wake the fishes. But I don't mind, no one is around to hear us. And even if they were, her lyrics of pleasure are music to my ears.

I haven't even tasted her yet, but I can see the gleam of her arousal between her legs in the moonlight. Slick and hot, I know she'll taste like the best dessert I've ever sunk into when I put my lips on her.

My lips come to hover right over her clit, and I breath a hot breathe on it.

"Cain, I need …"

"I know, baby."

And I lick, one long hot stroke of my tongue from the center of her all the way to the bundle of nerves strung tight.

She whimpers, as if it's the best pain and the best pleasure. I go at her again, slowly feasting on her until her hands are in my hair and she's crying out for release.

When she finally does come, with my name on her lips, that feeling surges through me again.

Invincible. Only this time, I know it applies to her and me.

29

HARPER

I wave to Grady and Paul as I pass them on the stairs. "Hey, guys."

They wave back at me. "'Sup?"

It's more of a rhetorical question, and I smile as I go down and they walk up. Cain's friends have become my friends by way of being in a relationship. And since I'd become his girlfriend, it seemed that everyone in school knew who I was, even teachers. I'd been freaked out the other day when his football coach, who was the head physical education teacher, had nodded his head to me during my gym class.

The bell was going to ring at any moment, and I did not want to be late to seventh period. As if it wasn't bad enough that I could barely focus with the images of Cain and me by the lake a couple of days ago swimming through my head.

"Do you think I can tap that after Cain? She has one sweet motherfucking rack." I hear Grady's voice lilt down from the top of the staircase.

They think I've exited the stairs, that I've gone down the hallway to my next class. I'm not sure what makes me stay, glued to the second to last step while they climb the ones above me, but I'm fixated to the spot.

"Nah, man, he has some weird territorial shit with that one. Plus, she wouldn't count toward your ten. Remember, no repeats was a rule. Or else we could just all fuck the same ten easy girls. We would know that they put out and then no one would win the competition. It would be a dead tie." Paul speaks in a hushed tone, but I can still hear them.

What the hell? What are they talking about? Competition?

"Oh yeah, you're right. He's so close to winning, just has to bag her. Whatever, I'm still trying for ten before graduation. Do threesomes count as two girls? Was that a rule?" Grady talks as they walk off, their voices fading.

Oh my God. Oh my God. A competition ... for what? Sex? That's sure what it sounded like. And Cain was close to winning? So I was ... what? Some medal to be hung around his neck?

My cheeks heat, because I knew it. And yet, I didn't want to get ahead of myself. I text Cain to meet me in the library. Five seconds later, he let me know he'd be there in three minutes and added a wink face. He thinks I want to make out. No wonder it was always about the physical with him.

All he was trying to do was fuck me and win some sick contest.

I walk among the stacks, waiting to see the tall, dark and handsome figure stroll through the door of the library. After about two minutes of pacing, he appears, smiling as he takes me in.

I don't wait for him, but walk farther back, all the way to the end of a row and around the corner, where no one will be able to hear or see us.

"Getting horny at school, huh? I knew you couldn't resist me, darlin', but this is a new level. I'm proud." He winks, and dives in to pull me close to his body.

I hold a hand against his chest, pushing back on the muscled force just a bit. "What is the ten girl competition?"

His eyes snaps up from where they were ogling my cleavage, and his entire body goes rigid, the hairs on his arms standing up.

Gotcha.

It's all I can think, I've caught him in some bold-faced lie that I don't even know what to make of yet. Cain opens his mouth and then closes it, like he's assessing how to proceed from here. Like he's formulating the lie that's going to come out of his mouth.

"Look, Harper—" he starts.

I cut him off, knowing full-well he can usually charm his way out of anything. "Don't lie to me. Don't you dare. What was I, just some kind of touchdown to you? Another thing you could score?"

Cain wrings his hands and then faces them up to me, as if praying for me to understand. "It was a stupid thing that we made a bet on freshman year. Way before I met you, baby. It ... it was all a dumb, stupid guy thing. And after I got to know you, I didn't even consider the competition anymore. You know how I feel about you."

My mouth drops open and I know I'm going to cry. "You have a competition with your friends to see who could have sex with ten girls first? And what, I was number ten? I was going to be your winning token? How could I be such an idiot!"

Cain goes to talk, but I cut him off again, tears now spilling down my cheeks, hot and angry.

"And what kind of person are you to make a bet like that? You think women are objects, that much is for sure. Who wants to use sex as a game? Someone who is a piece of shit, that's who!"

My voice is at an ear-splitting level, and a couple of people have poked their head into the row where Cain and I are fighting, but I can't even pay attention to them. Not with my heart literally breaking there between the shelves.

"Harper, calm down. I know it was wrong, it was so stupid and wrong. I'm sorry that I ever decided to take part in it. But that's before I met you. Before you showed me a different side, showed me that I was capable of caring for someone. Before I fell in love with you."

I whisper, gasping on my sobs, "Don't. Don't say those words to me. You don't care about me. I told you that I was in love with you and all you wanted to do was get in my pants. I can't believe I almost gave you that. I can't believe you told me you loved me, too."

Cain goes to wipe away a tear, and I jerk back. "Baby, please ... I stopped us the other night. I stopped us because I wanted to show you that you're more important to me than sex. Than anything. You and your heart, that's what I care about."

Tears slide down my cheeks. "Yeah well, you have an awful way of showing it. I can never trust you again."

"Harper—"

I can't bear to hear anymore. "No. Don't touch me. Don't talk to me. I never want to see you again."

"Baby ..."

I walk away from Cain, leaving him standing among the shelves in the back of the library.

It's impulsive, but I walk straight out of the library and through the back doors of school. I'm cutting class, but what matters more right now is that my heart was just crushed under the weight of a thousand lies. I couldn't possibly sit there and learn about the Civil War while trying to hold back tears.

The sobs wrack my body the entire way home.

30

HARPER

The week between the football championship and Thanksgiving sees the drama and gossip mill at Haven High School pushed to the max.

Apparently, someone overheard Cain and I arguing in the library, and after that, the talk spread like wildfire. About the competition ... and eventually, which girls had been marks in it. There was practically an alert sent out, girl wide over the entire student body, not to sleep with Cain or any of his friends.

While they were still the most popular guys in school, it was clear that they had a stain now, that the young females of our town were avoiding them.

I thought it was disgusting. Taking myself and my heart out of the equation, I couldn't wrap my mind around how someone could propose such a bet. That they got their kicks from it, from tallying up girls and banging anyone who was willing ... it was gross. It made me want to take a shower.

And I had. I'd practically scalded my skin. Knowing that Cain was a part of it, again taking my heart out of it, and his hands had been on me. I felt dirty, like there were spots of filth on me now that I couldn't get off.

When it came to my feelings for him ... that was a whole other issue entirely. Every time I started to think about it, my cheeks heated with shame and embarrassment. My heart would sink, the tears and bile rising up the back of my throat to form a mixed lump. He'd tricked me so deeply that I'd fallen in love with a boy who was incapable of anything but bedding girls blindly.

I'd known his reputation. I knew I had not been the first girl he'd wooed, or even the first one to slide her bra straps down her shoulders. But ... he'd pretended to care about me. Had asked questions, wanted to know about my books and my thoughts. He quoted classic authors to me, had held my hand when we jumped off the bridge together, had so tenderly held me that night at the lake.

Cain had stopped himself before we went too far. What kind of sick game was he playing that he acted like a gentleman to get me to fall farther into his trap? Was it so that I would finally give up the one thing I said I would wait to do? Because I have to admit, then his game had worked. I'd wanted to lose my virginity to him that night on the banks of the water.

I wept most nights, silently, the sobs wracking my shoulders as I hugged a pillow to my stomach. I couldn't go three seconds without thinking of him, or the way he had looked at me. I cried in the shower, I cried in the horse pastures where no one could see me. Mom and Grandma knew that something was wrong, but they hadn't prodded me too much. Hell, I barely showed up to dinner anymore. I just wasn't hungry.

At school, it was a mixed bag. Some of the popular kids still spoke to me, while most chose to ignore the weird new girl that Cain Kent had ... what? We hadn't dated. We hadn't had sex.

We were nothing. Not anymore.

I still had MK and Imogen, and at least it was the week

before a holiday, so most of the students and teachers were in that mode of just wanting to get the hell out of school.

The only thing that distracted me was marketing my book. I'd found more than a few blogs who wanted to help promote it after reading advanced copies, and I spent endless hours emailing more to ask politely if they'd like a review copy.

I made graphics and set up photo shoots for my slowly growing Instagram. I reached out to readers and read reviews on Goodreads, which sometimes backfired on me. I tried to stay positive and had decided for a publish date of early January. I wanted the book to get some traction with bloggers before I released it, so that maybe the word would be out there.

But when my work was done, and I'd trudged through homework and studying for actual school, the cloud of heartbreak loomed so low over my head that I could swear it was raining at all times.

He had broken me. Cain had done what no boy had done before. He had made me fall in love. So deeply and without a backward glance that I look back now at the stupid girl who had been convinced he was a good guy ... and I want to smack her.

The question I ask myself the most is, *would I always feel like this?*

Other people had been heartbroken before, and they were still living. Still standing. So when did this stop? When did my heart glue itself back together? When would the pit in my stomach cease to exist?

How could I possibly live with this gnawing desperation clinging to every bone and fiber?

If I could go back, I'd run the other way the first day I saw that boy get out of his Jeep.

31

CAIN

"I *am what you designed me to be. I am your blade. You cannot now complain if you also feel the hurt."*

These are the only words I've received from Harper in the last text she sent me. That was over two weeks ago, and she's cut off all communication since. With Thanksgiving coming and going, half days and holidays and midterms ... I hadn't seen much of her. But when I had, she looked past me.

As if I were dead. A ghost, a memory she'd erased from her brain.

Her *Great Expectations* quote gutted me, because she was right. I had designed our entire relationship on the premise of fucking her to win the competition.

And because of my own actions, I'd used her as the blade that had cut my heart in half, too. I could barely sleep these days, nothing held enjoyment for me. Not watching sports news and seeing highlights of myself and my team winning state. Not going to parties with my friends. Not even going to see Gramps.

Of course the rumors started the minute that she walked out of that library. Not that being in a relationship had stopped other girls from flirting with me, but it had been a nightmare now that I was single. Girls rubbing up against me, trying to walk to class with me, bringing me drinks at parties.

I wanted none of it. The only person I wanted was Harper.

And then of course, there was the rumor someone had started that I'd fucked her and then dumped her. That one was the worst of all. I tried to stem the bleeding, put a gag order on anyone I heard spreading that shit. But it didn't work. They all thought, from my past reputation, that I'd boned the new girl and then sent her crying once I broke her heart.

Twice, too, I'd had to threaten to beat the piss out of someone who was talking shit about her in my vicinity. At least it was nice to know that Harper still had MK, who shot me a death glare anytime she saw me in the hallway.

"Yo, Kent, are you even listening?" Paul hits me hard with the back of his hand to my pec.

It hadn't taken long for me to figure out that it had been my idiot friends blabbing their mouths about the competition around school that had fueled Harper to break up with me.

"No," I deadpan.

We were walking down Main Street, about to go try out the new taco place that had just opened up, except I couldn't figure out why I'd come in the first place. I wanted no part of being around this crew right now.

"He's still pissed off about the new girl. She won't ride his dick anymore." Grady raise his eyebrows and laughs.

"Eh, whatever, she's yesterday's garbage anyway. Cain wham bam, thank you ma'amed her." Emmitt holds his hand out to me for a fist bump.

I round on him, stopping our motley crew from moving any farther down the street. "Don't you ever speak about her like that again."

He holds his hands up. "Ease up, man. It's just a chick."

I run my hands through my hair, frustrated. "It's not just a chick. I love her."

Grady laughs like a hyena. "What?! Love? Who the fuck are you?"

I break off from them, knowing where I need to go. "Man, forget you guys."

Part of me doesn't even feel like explaining to them, because they won't get it. Hustling across the street, I walk toward the place I know I can go to find solace and advice.

Ten minutes later, I'm walking through the doors of Sons of America, and Nanette looks surprised to see me. "It's not Monday, honey."

"Does a guy need an excuse to visit his gramps?" I smile weakly at her.

She points down the hall. "He's in the recreation room, playing solitaire."

I walk toward it, knowing my way around the place because I was the grandson of the self-appointed mayor of the joint. When I enter the doorway of the rec room, I see a familiar figure hunched over at a table in the corner, cards laid out in front of him.

"I don't know how you play this game, it's so boring," I greet him.

He doesn't look up. "It's called skill and patience, two things that your teenage behind won't have for a long time, sonny."

I sit down in the chair next to his and watch him finish his game.

When he does, he looks up. "So, you have girl troubles, huh?"

My mouth drops open. "How did you know?"

Gramps chuckles. "Boy, I might be old, but I'm not blind. You have heartbreak written all over your face. What happened with Harper? I like her, she's a very nice girl."

"I screwed it up," I grumble.

"Well, what did you do?"

I'm definitely not telling him about the competition. He is blood, but he still may slap me upside the head. "I told some friends some uh … things about our relationship. Things I should have kept between us. And she got upset, called me a liar, broke up with me."

There, that kind of summed it up for him.

Gramps' face contorts into a scowl. "You kissed and told, didn't you? That's the opposite of what a gentleman does."

"I know." I sigh, "What can I do to get her back?"

He studies me. "One time, after we'd been married for five years, I did something that hurt your grandmother. Now, I'm not going to get into it, but you should know that I had been a real jerk. And to make up for it, I groveled. You need to perfect your grovel, because if you love a woman, you'll be doing it a lot. You need to be damn sorry, and then kiss the ground she walks on. Because women, they are the superior gender, even if we want to be stubborn about it. Apologize, because I can tell that you love this girl. You're all torn up over her."

I was surprised, I'd always thought that they'd had the perfect marriage. "I can't believe you two fought."

"Everyone fights, Cain. It's what you do when you're in love. You fight with each other, for each other, and against the world."

His poetic words renew a sense of fight inside of *me*. Even though I screwed up, so badly, with Harper, I was going to grovel. And then I was going to fight. For us.

"Now, that hand looks brutal. You need to call your father, and get it looked at."

I hadn't even been holding my hand out for him, yet he'd known it was hurt. "I swear, some days I think you are psychic."

32

CAIN

As if my heart wasn't broken enough for the rest of my body, my finger was still throbbing every second of the day.

I sit on the table of one of the best sports medicine doctors in Texas, as he pulls and pushes at my hand. He might as well have been slicing daggers into my fingertips.

"Ouch ..." I wince.

"Yeah, I think that finger is broken. I'm going to have to splint it, and I'll give you a cortisone shot before that. Hopefully with it immobile and putting you out of pain, will give it time to heal."

I look up at the ceiling, push out a breath and try to swallow the tears collecting in my throat. "I'm going to have to report this to my university, aren't I?"

The doctor, a guy with sandy brown hair in his mid-forties, sighs and his mouth drops into a frown. "I'm afraid so. I'm also going to have to give them my report, but if I were you, I'd call them first. I'll give you time to do that. Luckily, you have almost nine months to recover from this, which will be more than enough time. You should go see the orthopedic surgeon to get a second opinion about surgery. I've looked to make sure everything in there is attached and straight before we set it in the splint, but you'll need to get an MRI. And I can give you the number for the surgeon."

The words surgery and recovery echo in my ears, and I try to bite down the bile working its way up my throat. Even though it was a minor injury, my brain still rattles with fear knowing that my hand is my golden goose.

I leave the doctor's office with a splint and a referral to an orthopedic surgeon. My hand is numb from the shot the doctor dispensed into it, and I figure I have to call Dad with the news.

As I'm crossing Main Street, I look into the alley beside the coffee shop. The one where Harper let me touch her for the first time. Where she gave her trust to me.

I was a fucking idiot.

I shake my head and keep moving, until I see a flash of white-blond from the window inside the cafe. There she is, in her favorite spot by the window, the warmth and coziness of the shop making my bones chill as I stand in the shade of a cold December afternoon.

Harper is intensely typing on her laptop, the one that looks like it had come straight out of the nineties. I wonder, offhand, if she has published her novel. She had let me read only snippets of it, and before I'd thoroughly ruined our relationship with my lie, I'd been begging her for more. I argued that she couldn't let me read part of a mystery and not get to know the ending.

Either way, I'd been searching Amazon in the time we'd been apart, to see if Harper Posy was a published author yet. I planned to buy the book as soon as it came out.

Gramps' words hit me right where it hurt. I'd screwed up, but I also hadn't fought for her. I haven't done a thing to show her how much I love her, that I would take bombs, bullets and bad guys on for her.

Losing Harper has taught me that there are more important

things in life than fame, fortune and football. I wasn't sure why I was thinking in such alliterative phrases, but I guess heartbreak would do that to a guy.

Before her, I'd been resting on my laurels, tapping into my athletic talent and playing around with girls. I hadn't wanted anything serious, had pushed it away with my complex about females leaving me. But once I'd lost Harper, it was like something inside of me broke. That shell I'd been protecting my heart with had cracked and crumbled to ash.

Why the hell have I been running away from one of the best things that has ever happened to me? I sabotaged our relationship with that stupid fucking competition, and then after she found out, I tried to lie about it.

I hadn't tried to talk to her, not seriously, since our split. I'd half-assed begging, had tried to talk to her girlfriends, had sent sappy, sad text messages. But I'd been consumed with my heartbreak. I hadn't really considered what it would take to heal her splintered love.

Staring at her through that coffee shop window, I know that I need to prove it to her. To show that I am going to fight for us.

33

HARPER

Holidays weren't a big deal when it was only you and your mother living in a trailer in a part of the world where it didn't even snow.

Our Christmas in Florida had consisted of opening one present each and then eating Mom's braised chicken at the kitchen table, where the tiniest lit up tree from Walmart sat.

But in Texas, they did everything big. And even though you'd think Grandma was too grouchy to deck the hall ... man, did she deck them.

Tinsel, ornaments, even cutting down our own enormous tree on the outskirts of the property. Grandma grew evergreens specifically for the purpose of having a fresh one in her house for Christmas. She had carols on all the time, since Thanksgiving that was the only music we'd been allowed to listen to at home. And she'd warned us that we better bring our present game, because she didn't mess around.

"Was she always like this growing up?" I whispered to Mom one day when we'd been helping Grandma make a dozen batches of Christmas cookies.

"Not as intense, but I think after Grandpa died, she thought she had to uphold the traditions for both of them," she'd whispered back.

We were spending Christmas Day just the three of us, with church in the morning and a big old feast in the afternoon. But for Christmas Eve, we'd been invited to spend the day with Michael and Annabelle, and my mom had accepted before I could make up some excuse of why I couldn't go.

So here I am, sitting on Annabelle Mills' couch with a glass of eggnog, trying not to bolt out the door. I would try hard for Mom, but this just isn't natural.

"We chopped it right down. Well, I laid on the ground while Annabelle held the tree, probably texting as I struggled with a blunt hacksaw." Michael laughs, putting his hand on my mother's knee.

I look down into my drink. Even though it's Christmas and it's supposed to be a festive time with family, I can't help but let the sorrow wash in. I think about Cain every day. And even though I should hate him ... I still love him so much.

It feels like there is a gaping wound in the middle of my chest that only I can see. How I'm supposed to function, much less get through the school year in the same building as him, I'm not sure how that's going to happen.

Michael asks Mom to help him in the kitchen with dinner, and Grandma goes to check out the collection of hunting magazines that Michael keeps in his study.

Grandma and Mom definitely know there is something going on with me, but they've been kind enough to not ask about the constantly red eyes or mounds of tissues in my trash can. They don't ask why Cain doesn't come around anymore, because I have a feeling they know. I'm not sure they realize how badly he broke my heart, but they've given me space and I'm glad. I'm not sure I can even formulate words to describe the kind of anguish my heart and pride are in.

"He really does love you." Annabelle is staring at me from the loveseat across the room.

My mouth goes dry. "Excuse me?"

"Cain. He might have done an asshole thing, but he's a guy. They can be assholes." She shrugs. "But, if you're hurting as bad as he is right now, you might consider forgiving him."

I'm stunned. Actually, literally shocked. The same girl who had tried to ruin my life in Haven from day one was trying to tell me to get back together with my ex-boyfriend. The one she'd called dibs on and then trashed me to.

"I'm sorry, this is none of your business." I stare her down, too numb and heartbroken to put up with whatever game she's playing.

"I know you don't want to hear anything from me. I know I've been a bitch ... and maybe it's just because I didn't want to see Cain happy with anyone. But now that you guys are broken up ... part of me just feels bad. Prior to everyone's belief, I'm not so bad. Damaged, yes. But not bad. And I'm telling you, that boy loves you."

My arms cross over my chest. "Did he tell you this?"

Annabelle's face breaks into a small smile. "He didn't have to. He's barely spoken to his friends in a month, proof that he feels guilty as all hell for starting that dumb competition. Cain also hasn't shown up to any parties since you split, and he won't even look in another girl's direction. He hurt his hand for you, broke his finger punching Josiah to defend your honor even though it could have meant the end of his career before it started. He also has been radio silent on social media or texting, and the way he looks at you ..."

"How does he look at me?" I lean forward on the couch, not caring if I seem desperate in this moment.

Annabelle isn't looking at me, but out the window. "Like he'll break into a million pieces if he can't be next to you. Like if he was in a desert and there was a choice between you or water, he'd pick you."

She looks back at me, focused. "When a guy looks at you like that, you need to recognize it. Don't take it for granted."

My heart is thumping in my chest. While her advice is sound, I have a feeling it comes from a deeper place.

Annabelle takes a sip of her eggnog, and then opens her mouth to speak again. "You know that he's having surgery today, right?"

A pang echoes in my heart. If we had still been together, I would have been there. I would have brought him chicken soup, or a cheeseburger with extra hot sauce, his favorite. I can't describe the feeling that runs over my skin. Desperation? Anguish? But the pit in my stomach makes me feel bereft, as if I've left him hurting instead of the other way around.

"I hope he's okay." It's a moment of weakness, and it comes out in a whisper.

"I'm serious, Harper. He didn't even think twice about punching that guy's lights out to defend you. This could end his career, and Cain hadn't thought twice. That is love. Before you, all he cared about was football. I wouldn't say this just to pull your leg ... he really has changed."

I cleared my throat, not wanting to dig into my emotions any further. "You know, maybe you aren't all that bad."

She shrugs. "I mean, I think we're going to have to get used to each other. Those two lovebirds won't stop making mistletoe eyes at each other."

I chuckle. "Yeah, but they're happy. Maybe we'll get lucky enough one day to be as happy as them."

Annabelle looks at me, smiling a conspiratorial grin. "Maybe we will. In any case, I think you have an opportunity to be that happy right now."

34

CAIN

I spend Christmas in the hospital, in and out of the drug haze they'd supplied me with after having surgery on my broken finger.

Luckily, I wasn't alone. Dad has come home to see me through the procedure and recovery, and even though he is still pissed that I played through it during the state championship game, I was so happy to have him in Haven for the holiday.

On the television was *A Wonderful Life*, and Dad and I were eating chicken fried steak that he'd gotten in takeout containers from the local diner.

"I forgot how much I missed this place." Dad smiles at me as he finishes up his dinner, placing it on the rolling cart near my hospital bed.

"The hospital?" I chuckle.

Dad rolls his eyes at me. "No, you goof. Haven, I missed Haven. And I missed you."

"I missed you, too." It was Christmas, and I was on drugs. I was allowed to be corny.

"Did you know that Gramps elected himself the mayor of Sons of America?" Dad laughs.

I crack up. "Yes. He makes the rounds in his wheelchair, waving like he's the king in his carriage or something. Tries to settle disputes, like if the air conditioner is too high or low, and which nineteen fifties musical they should screen at movie night."

"He is in his glory, there. Misses Mom, though." Dad sighs. "I think we all do."

"She's still up there, scowling down at us about the choices she deems bad," I joke with him.

But really, it's not a joke. I know that woman is up there, giving me a death glare about what happened between Harper and I. Stupidly, I thought maybe she would be in my hospital room, waiting for me, holding my hand next to the side of the bed as I woke up. I thought someone would have gotten word to her, and wishful thinking had tainted my drug-addled brain.

But, she wasn't here. I'd texted her a Merry Christmas, as I'd texted her something every single day since we've been broken up. But, just like every other day, she hasn't responded.

I just want to get out of here so I can fight for us, just like Gramps had told me to do.

My father smiles, and a silence settles over us. He's in street clothes, which seems so weird to me. Of course I've seen my father in jeans and T-shirts, but I'm just so much more used to seeing him in uniform. In plain clothes, he looks like a normal, average guy. He has muscles, but wasn't as imposing as a bigwig in the army.

"Well, I hope she's going to be smiling at me when I tell you about the decision I've made." Dad wrings his hands.

I look at him, teasing, "What, that you're finally going to let your hair grow out? No more buzz cuts."

"I took a desk job. I'm hanging up my combat boots and settling into a cushy teaching position at the nearby base." He stares at me, watching the words filter through my ears.

I blink. "You ... you're not going out on another tour?"

He shakes his head. "I'm not. I have to be home to watch my boy play college football. Plus, I don't need to work for much longer. You're going to buy me a house when you become rich and famous."

I didn't care how old I was, that I was a man myself ... I lean forward and hug him. "It's a deal."

We embrace for the first time in a long time, and when I pull away first, there are tears in Dad's eyes. "But you know, football isn't life, bud."

We both stare down at my finger, which is wired in a contraption and bandaged to high heaven. "I'm beginning to understand that, believe me."

"I kind of had a feeling you were. I hope this has taught you that playing a sport as a career is so fleeting. I know how risky a career can be, maybe not in the athletic field, but I do know. There are so many more important things than fame and money, son. Family, that's number one. Happiness, that's number two. I don't want you to run from both of those things, like me. They are essential, and I need to start paying them more attention than I do my career. I hope you keep that in mind as you start yours."

I nod. "You didn't raise me to be ignorant of that, Dad. I want you to know that. It's starting to sink in, with this surgery but also with college on the horizon. Football is my dream, but it can vanish in a second. I don't want to be left holding the bag, miserable, if it doesn't work out."

Dad clears his throat, clearly emotional. "Jeez, did you get smart while I was away or what?"

We both just look at each for a beat, realizing that while he is coming home, I am on my way out of town. Life is going to be very different, come this time next year. But it isn't a bad different. Life ebbs and flows like the lake on the shores of my favorite spot, and you just have to go with it.

"So, should we sneak some extra Jell-O from the nurses for dessert?" Dad starts to clear our plates.

"Only if it's the red kind. Green is nasty. Go get us extra, charm them, Dad. I saw the blond one checking you out earlier." I wasn't lying, she really had been checking him out.

"Oh, yeah?" He looks surprised. "Maybe I can get a cookie or two, then."

35

CAIN

Two days after Christmas, I drive to Harper's house with my bandaged up hand and still broken heart.

Cautiously, I park, walk up the steps, and knock on the door. I know that Harper probably won't answer it once she sees who is standing on her front porch, but I figure I have to give it a shot.

Instead of the girl I love, though, I am greeted by her grandmother.

Who has a big fat scowl on her face.

"I knew you'd come around here eventually."

Blanche reaches toward the wall to the left of her, but because I'm standing on the front porch, I don't see what she's trying to get.

Until there is a shotgun pointed straight at my nose.

"Woah! Mrs. Posy, I ..." I put my hands up, hoping to keep my skull intact long enough to talk to Harper.

"You what? Broke my granddaughter's heart? Are an asshole? A little shit. I should pop you right now, boy. It would be worth going to jail for."

I'd heard you should never mess with Mama Posy, but damn,

I hadn't expected this. She was Texas through and through. My balls had just about shrunk up into my body when someone started shouting behind her.

"Mama! Put that down!" Clara appears at the door and grabs the gun, the barrel swinging this way and that as they wrestle over it.

I jump down, stumbling over three steps until I am standing in the dirt. Well, more like cowering away from these two women who were about to put holes in me or themselves.

Harper's mom finally takes the gun away, setting it down inside and blowing out a breath while shaking her head.

"You're off your damn rocker," she mutters to her mother.

"Somebody has to teach that boy a lesson," Grandma Posy harrumphs.

Clara swings her gaze to me, observing and judging. "Yeah, I heard what you did, Cain Kent. Hell of a stunt you pulled on my daughter. But I'm going to guess that if you're here, you feel worse than she does right now. As you should."

I scuff my sneaker in the dirt. "Yes, ma'am. I just want to talk to her."

"We ain't her daddy, God rest his soul, but we could still beat the piss out of you. And clearly, we know how to shoot the piss out of you, too, if that's what we wanted to do."

She's threatening me, and I gulp. "Yes, ma'am."

"You're not going to make a mistake with my daughter again, correct?"

"No, ma'am." I look her in the eye, my mood solemn.

"And you're in love with her?" This was the test, her eyebrow raises, waiting to see what I will say.

I angled my chin up. "Yes, ma'am."

A beat passes, and they both stare at me. Then her mom speaks. "Good man. She's out in the pasture by the woods, you can find her there."

"What?!" Blanche protests, but her daughter places her hand on her mother's arm.

"You tried to stop young love once, look how well that turned out. If it's meant to be, it will find a way. Life is about mistakes. It's how we correct them that matters."

She looks at me when she says that last part, and I take off in a run out toward the back of the Posy property.

Harper is almost a mile out, sitting in the fields alone, her blond hair gleaming under the setting sun. She's looking off into the horizon, and doesn't hear or see me. I take the moment to admire her, to digest her with my eyes. In a couple of minutes, she could completely reject me forever. So right then, I just wanted to observe the girl I love, in her peaceful, relaxed state.

My sneakers clomp over the grass, my hands shake and my heart pounds so loudly that I think it's what makes Harper turn her head.

Those blue eyes widen in surprise, and I talk before she can tell me to get the hell away from her.

"I loved her against reason, against promise, against peace, against hope, against happiness, against all discouragement that could be." I quoted *Great Expectations* to her.

Sitting down beside her, I rise up on my knees so I can hold my hands out in forgiveness. "For a long time, I thought that love between a girl and a boy didn't exist. Every woman in my life has left, and besides, I have places I want to go. I couldn't have a relationship that would tether me, tie me down."

Harper looks like she wants to speak, but I hold a finger up, needing her to hear all of this.

"And because of that mentality, I pushed every single girl away. I made up dumb competitions and didn't take into account people's feelings. I was an asshole, and it was a low, low thing to do. But ... then I met you. And as much as I, stupidly, thought that being with you threatened where I wanted to go, I couldn't push you away. I kept falling harder for you; the way you talked with me, how smart and funny you were. And God, Harper, you're just beautiful ... sometimes I find myself staring at you and I lose track of time. It wasn't until reality hit me square in the jaw, when you broke up with me, that I realized that having you in my life wasn't a tether. You weren't tying me down, you were helping me fly. I love you, and I'm not going anywhere if you're not by my side to do it with me."

When I finish pouring my heart out, I look at her. Harper's eyes are sparkling with unshed tears, and she's so close to touching one of my outstretched hands that I have to fight every nerve ending in me not to do it for her.

"You hurt me. And you lied. I want you to know that both of those will never be okay for you to do again." Her expression isn't exactly open, but it's not closed

"Again?" My voice is the definition of hope.

"I love against reason." She shrugs, those beautiful lips turning up in a small smile. "I never had a chance when it came to you, Cain. But, I also have places I want to go. We aren't going to hold each other back, especially at such a young age. We both have growing up to do, but I want to do it with you."

Finally, her small hand meets mine, and our fingers lace together.

"How did I get so lucky?"

Harper tilts her head. "I'm not sure it's luck. I think that we both see in each other, something that makes us whole."

"Babe, you put into words feelings that I could never even try to describe. So yes, you understand me like no one ever will."

I bend to kiss her. This kiss, not our first in the least, feels new. It holds promises and whispers of the future. This kiss feels like we're starting off on a journey toward something so much bigger than this little town.

36

HARPER

The clock is ticking down, an hour to go, as Taylor Swift shakes her stuff in front of the audience in Times Square.

Someone has rigged up a giant projection screen in The Atrium, the sight of tonight's New Year's Eve party for pretty much all of the students at Haven High school. It's true, the last time I was here, I wasn't really even inside this building, but the party happening right now is a whole other level.

Girls in sequined party dresses or blinged out cowboy boots, boys in all varying shades of dress ... from those joking around by wearing tuxedos, to Cain, who is in a nice button down and jeans. I'd gone for a simple black dress, but one that showed a little cleavage. All night, I couldn't keep from blushing because Cain couldn't keep his eyes from wandering down to the V at my chest.

"Take a shot with me pleaseee!" MK comes over, looping an arm around my neck.

"No thanks, I'm not really drinking tonight. But, hey, what a novel concept, I'm still having fun!"

"Spare me the after school special lecture." Annabelle walks up, rolling her eyes.

"Just looking out for you, sister." Sarcasm dripping from my voice.

She shudders. "God, who would have thought that the new girl will someday, probably, become my sister? I get first pick of bridesmaid dress ... I have to look better than you."

Obviously, supermodel Anna would look better than me in anything, but I didn't care. We were getting along ... or well, we had this kind of fun banter with each other. I don't think we'll ever hug through the tough times or braid each other's hair, but we were getting to a place of friendship, and that was all right with me.

"She was my friend first, don't forget that. Hey, maybe I can be like an honorary sister," Mary-Kate slurred, but the smile on her face was too goofy and sweet not to laugh with her.

"Of course you can." I hug her waist.

Anna blows out a breath. "God, are we starting some kind of YaYa sisterhood or some shit?"

"Oh, come do a shot with me, queen bee. Let your hair down." MK winks at me and starts to pull Annabelle away.

I stand in the middle of the warehouse, mesmerized by all of the light and noise. There has to be hundreds of kids here, all moving and dancing and talking. They were bright and bubbly, everyone teetering on the edge of an old year and about to be plunged into a new one. And even though I stood alone, I didn't feel it.

I'd become a part of this close-knit town, with its typical Texas flair and quirky townspeople. When we'd first moved back to Mom's hometown, I hadn't been expecting a thing. I'd wanted to keep my head down, to get through the school year without attachments and then float on from this place, almost as if I'd never been here at all.

But it had sucked me in. With its charm and heat, the dust from the gravel roads has become imbedded so deep in my skin that now, I knew I'd always be a part of Haven. And it would always be a part of me.

The biggest part, the one that would always remain close now, is staring at me from across the room. I can feel his eyes on my body, moving up from toes to knees to waist to breasts to chin to eyes. And when they meet, his green and mine blue, a spark ignites between us. Even though there is a mass of bodies in the way, I can feel his gaze like the warmth of a thousand suns.

Cain smiles, almost shy, and waves. I wiggle my fingers back, and it feels like we could be strangers meeting for the first time.

It has been less than a week since our reconciliation, but now that we are together again, it feels like no time at all has passed. We've been spending nearly every waking moment of what was left of winter break together, and some of the sleeping parts. Since his dad had left right after he'd gotten out of the hospital, to wrap up some of his tour duties before he could come home for good, I'd slept a night or two at Cain's house.

We fooled around, which was incredible, but mostly I just loved the feeling of falling asleep wrapped completely in him. I wasn't sure which felt better, nodding off in his arms, or waking up in them.

We have spent most of tonight together, but have broken off at times, going to talk to our separate friends. But we did dance, never straying too far, both of our heads swiveling to check the other's proximity pretty much every minute.

And now he is walking toward me, those long legs and commanding presence parting the sea of people between us while his eyes never leave mine. Lord, he is handsome. I remember the first day I saw him, how in awe of this golden boy I was. I was astonished by him then, but even more so now.

Because I know that underneath the bad boy exterior, the pouty lips and rugged bone structure, is a heart that was more tender than even Cain liked to admit.

"Fancy seeing you here. Do you have a midnight kiss lined up?" His arms wind around my waist, and he practically picks me up off the floor.

I tilt my head, pretending to think. "I do, but if you can sweet talk me into it, I might let you beat him to it."

"Oh, my lucky night." He winks, and then steals my lips, catching them in a heated, growl of a kiss.

When we break away, to a wolf whistle or two, I smile up at him. "How many drinks have you had?"

Cain holds up three fingers in a scout's honor salute. "One beer, my lady. I'm holding to our pact. One drink, and then champagne at midnight. See, I can be a responsible adult."

I swat his butt in a playful move. "The only responsible thing about you is me."

Those green eyes light up. "That's true, but I like you bossy."

We'd made a pact before coming to this party that we wouldn't drink much. Both of us wanting to keep a clear head and enjoy the night with each other, no alcohol tainting it. I'd told him he could have a beer with the guys, and we could both drink bubbly to toast at midnight.

After dancing a little and chatting with his group of friends, whom Cain seems to be warming back up to after the entire competition coming to light, it was time to count down to the new year.

"Five, four, three, two, ONE!" The entire Atrium shakes with the tenor of voices screaming the final second of two thousand eighteen.

The countdown clock hits triple zeros, and all of a sudden, the room goes quiet. People are kissing, friends are hugging, a lot of the jocks are chugging beers. *Way to start a new year*, I think sarcastically.

But all thoughts cease when Cain pulls me in for a kiss. It's long and slow, mind-numbing, time-stopping. It is celebratory and passionate all in the same breath.

It's after midnight. We left last year behind, and all of the ugliness that had come with it was washed away. Wasn't that what New Year's was about? Turning the page, starting fresh?

I want to do that. And I want to do that by getting rid of the only thing still standing between Cain and me.

My virginity.

37

HARPER

Half an hour after midnight, we pull into the driveway at Cain's house.

After the new year started, the party was still going strong, but some of the celebratory buzz had washed off for the two of us, and we just wanted to be alone. So he'd asked if I would sleep over, and of course I'd said yes.

Cain kills the headlights and turns the car off, turning to me in the dark and cupping my face before we both get out and walk in through the front door. He holds my hand, neither of us speaking, and I have a feeling that the same thoughts that are running through my head are running through his.

I speak up, knowing that I have to take the lead on this if I want it to happen. "I want you."

Cain's eyes widen, and his mouth forms an O. "You're sure? I want you to be absolutely sure."

I nod. "I want you to be my first. I want you to be my only, really. I love you, Cain. I told you that I'd be ready to have sex when I was in love, and I am."

My fingers feel the quickening of his pulse at his wrist, and I see it the moment that silky curtain of nerves rolls over his body.

"I don't want to mess this up for you. I want to make you feel good, not pain."

I gulp, scared about that part. "You will. I've been told it's natural for it to hurt a little, but I promise I won't hold it against you."

His laugh is low at my joke, and he breathes out a sigh. "Okay."

We walk up the stairs together to his bedroom, kissing lightly as we mount the steps. My heartbeat is thrumming in my brain, my lungs feel like they can't take in enough air. In my head, I'm calm and resolved in my decision. But between the arousal licking up my thighs and my racing heart, my body is fluctuating between panic and anticipation.

Stepping over the threshold of Cain's bedroom, he refrains from flicking on the lights. Drawing the curtains all the way open, moonlight pools in around our feet.

Slowly, we undress each other. The zipper of my dress splintering in the silence. The brush of his shirt against the smattering of hair on his chest. Both of our shoes, slowly toed off while Cain dusts light kisses down my collarbone. My dress is peeled past my hips and kicked gently across the floor. His boxer shorts sliding down, revealing every naked inch of him.

When we're down to our flesh, he wraps me up in him, the scent of spring fresh deodorant and the mint of the gum he had been chewing invading my nose. Goose bumps spring up on my body as Cain trails his fingertips all over it, from the round of my butt to the bones of my hips to my peaked nipples.

He walks us to the bed, where I scoot backward until he can crawl over me. I think he's going to come kiss me, but he stops midway up my body, his lips curving to the inside of my thigh with a wicked smile.

"Oh." It's all I can say as he begins to move his mouth, wetting my skin and leaving it tattooed with his brand.

Cain's mouth feasts on my core, leaving me panting and wound so tight that I think I might fracture from the pleasure. I'm more slick than I've ever been there, and when he pushes a thick finger in at the same time that his teeth nip at the swollen bud of my center, I moan so loud that I could have woken the dead.

Before I can reach that sought after cliff edge though, Cain and his long, lean arms are tenting over me. I'm vaguely aware of him rolling on a condom, how he got that so smoothly without fumbling, I don't know. But I'm staring into his eyes, both of us trying to speak without words.

This is a big moment.

Are you ready?

Yes. I love you.

I love you, too. His eyes shutter close for a brief moment and then open, blazing.

I brace myself, trying to stay calm but knowing this invasion will probably hurt. I spread my legs as wide as they'll go and then wrap my hands around Cain's back. I always thought of having sex as more of a metaphorical thing, but now that I'm about to do it, I actually see how natural it is. How he will fit with me, how we will physically perform the act of making love. It's the most intimate way that two people who love each other can express that feeling.

"Ahh ..." I can't help but cry out in pain when Cain pushes in, the rigidness of him splitting me in half.

I feel the pain everywhere, radiating from the inside out.

He pushes a lock of hair from my forehead and leans down, looking deep into my eyes. "Breathe, baby."

I do, gritting through my teeth. And slowly, the pain subsides. It gives way to a flood of feeling. There is a tinge of soreness, fullness ... but as Cain starts to stroke slowly, my entire body feels like it's one big nerve ending. I'm sparking, a fever spreading from my toes to the roots of my hair.

I grip the back of his neck and tentatively flex my hips every time he strokes, the sensation so good that it makes me whimper. I'm dangerously close to coming apart at the seams.

"I. Love. You. So. Much," Cain growls through his teeth, and I see for the first time just how much he's holding back.

"Let go. You won't hurt me." I kiss him, tasting the sweat from his cheek.

He grunts and starts to really move, his hips slapping against mine. Something deep within me starts to vibrate, expand and buzz with so much pleasure that I can't think. I only feel, only Cain.

The orgasm floats over me, an airy feeling that makes the hairs on my skin stand up and my muscles lose all control of themselves. Cain buries his face in my shoulder, mouthing my name and drawing it into my skin with his lips. His weight on top of me only makes the climax sweeter.

We lie like that for a long time, maybe the entire night ... I'm not even sure that the world is moving. It might have just up and stopped spinning.

I've lost it, maybe sooner than I thought I would, but I don't regret a thing.

Because I've gained so much more.

38

CAIN

"Come on, babe, just press it."

Harper's hand rests on her laptop, her knee bouncing up and down in time with, what I was guessing, her heartbeat.

We sit at the kitchen table in her house, Blanche and Clara standing at the counter preparing sandwiches for lunch.

"Aw, come on, child, just do it already." Blanche blows a breath out and gives her granddaughter her sternest look.

I cover her shaking knee with my hand and squeeze, hoping that it will calm her nerves.

"I know, I know ... it's just, there is no going back after this. Will people even buy it? And if they do, will they like it? What if I get a bad review?"

Her mom turns around. "And what if you don't publish it? Guess what? You'll never know any of those answers then. Do it now, or we'll hold your hands back and Cain will do it for you."

I press my lips to her forehead and watch her cheeks turn pink. I'll never tire of that blush, I've craved it since the day we met. "You can do this, babe."

She takes a deep breath, checks the details on the setup page about four more times, and then scrolls. And clicks publish now.

"Oh my God!" she squeals, hiding her eyes.

A tiny box pops up on the screen that tells her it may take forty-eight to seventy-two hours for the book to be available online, and then it flashes onto a screen where it says her book is in review.

"I can't believe it's out in the universe. That I'm going to be an actual, real published author." Harper turns to look at all of us.

Her mom and grandma start clapping and I join in, whooping and hollering.

Bending toward her, I kiss her cheek. "I'm so proud of you, baby."

Clara and Blanche come over, attacking her with kisses until she giggles. "We are, too."

Clara stands up and starts to cry happy tears. "Oh, I can't wait to buy my copy. I'm so excited."

"All right, Mom, hold your horses. It's not even published yet." Harper rolls her eyes, but smiles.

"Let's go get some ice cream to celebrate." I want to get her alone, but mostly I don't want her sitting in front of the computer refreshing it a hundred times over the next hour.

"Are you crazy? It's freezing out." She shivers.

Harper is adorable in her sweater, and it only makes me want to get her out of it more. Since we'd started having sex, I was like a crazed animal. I couldn't even have her in the same hundred yards of me without wanting to jump her. Feeling her, naked against me, made me an insatiable person. She fits perfectly with me, our bodies move together like waves in an ocean ... running one into the next into the next.

I have to bite the inside of my cheek to stop from hauling her off right now. How had I never known how good sex could be when you were in love with someone? I was a fool. But then again, it wouldn't have been right with anyone but Harper. I'd been waiting for her, I just hadn't known it.

"Then hot chocolate. We'll get hot chocolate." I take her hand and shake gently, inviting her to stand up.

"Yeah, you should get out. No use loitering around here, you'll know on your cell phone when it goes up anyway. Kids know everything these days from those cell phones." Blanche shakes her head.

Harper relents, and I drive us into town, walking to her favorite, and the only, coffee shop on Main Street. I buy us two hot chocolates and she picks her table by the window, where I join her with the steaming mugs.

"Thanks for getting me out, I needed this." She smiles at me as she cups her drink, a little bit of chocolate foam dusting her upper lip.

I lean across the table and use my thumb to wipe it off, loving the way she looks at me when I do. "I know what you need. Studying you is my favorite subject."

"What next? You're going to tell me I'm your desk and you need to do homework on me." She rolls her eyes at the corny sex joke.

"You know I only use my greatest pickup lines on you, darlin'." I wink. "So, what's the plan for the next book?"

Harper laughs. "I just finished this one, can't you give me a minute?"

I reach for her hand. "I can give you a minute, but just one. Because I know that this is your dream, so I'm going to push you to be the very best that you can at it. You told me that this was what you wanted to do, and I know a little something about giving two hundred percent. Even if I sound pushy sometimes, just know I only have your best interests in mind."

Her eyes crinkle. "Thanks, babe."

"Throwing babes around, huh? I like the nickname. Keep it coming." I take a sip of my hot chocolate and ask the one question I've been scared to pose until now. "So, with the book published now ... what will you do after graduation?"

She runs her free hand through her hair. "Well, I have to see how much money it makes first. That will largely make my decision. But ... if it does well, I want to use the money to travel. Just me, my laptop and the world."

My heart drops, because I know that is what's best for her, but I don't want to let her go. I love her, and I have to set her free. I still have a couple of months with Harper, this means, and I shouldn't have that in the back of my mind for all of them ... but I know I will.

"So, what will happen with us?" I sound so sensitive, but I don't care about being vulnerable with her.

Harper smiles. "Well, you don't think you're going to get rid of me that quickly, do you? I'm not letting those college girls anywhere near you."

My heart stops beating. "What do you mean?"

"I'm not a millionaire, I can't travel every day like an Instagram model. And I told you, I want to go with you. I want to share our journeys together. I want to watch you play collegiate football and get drafted, I want to be the one you throw in the air when you win a Super Bowl."

"So, you want to come with me to Austin?"

Harper nods. "I want to be there a majority of the time. And sometimes I'll travel. We'll have our own lives, but we'll do them together."

How the hell had I gotten this girl? How the hell did she know exactly what I needed? That when I got to college, I would need to balance football and a relationship. What Harper has proposed sounded like the best of both worlds.

"You're the only one I'd want to do this with."

And she was. She might have been the tenth girl, but she was the only. The only one who mattered. The only one who had ever broken me open and taught me how to feel.

The only one who I would ever love.

EPILOGUE

HARPER

Two Years Later

The Uber I took from the airport can't move fast enough.

My feet are tapping on the carpeted floor of the car, my hand clutching my phone, checking the time repeatedly.

"Is there any way you could go a little faster?"

"Lady, the game traffic is thicker than mud on a pig. There ain't no way I'm getting through this fast."

Opening up Google Maps, I track how far the stadium is from my location right now. Only about half a mile ... I could run that. Not well and I'd look like an uncoordinated chicken, but if I didn't sprint it, I would miss the start of the game.

"All right, I'm getting out. Thanks for the ride." I hop out, weaving my way over onto the sidewalk.

"Give me five stars!" The driver calls after me.

That's the least of my worries right now, but I'll do it eventually. I knew it was a bad idea to fly home from Vienna this morning. Cain had said it was fine, and it would have been ... except that my flight had gotten delayed and I was almost going to miss the opening kickoff of his sophomore year season.

Last year, he had redshirted until the starting quarterback had gotten hurt halfway through the season. Then Cain had come in, brought his college in the cute city of Austin all the way to the playoffs before they lost. Despite that, he was being talked about as the next coming of Jesus, and of course the entire state of Texas, as well as most of the national league fans, are obsessed with him.

As they should be ... I'd never expected any less. But this was his first game in the first season that he'd won the starting quarterback job fair and square. And if I didn't pick up my pace, I was going to miss it.

Cain and I have been together for almost three years now, two of those while he's been in college. And I'd been ... well, I'd been doing my author thing. We had done what we said we would, living our lives separately but together. He had football and the limelight, much of which I shied away from. Even if there had been a couple of pieces on the Internet tying Cain Kent to bestselling suspense author Harper Posy.

And while he was being Mr. Athlete, I was off at least a week or two every other month, writing in the cities of the worlds. Or sometimes, even, off the map. The trip I'd taken to the Swiss Alps, where I'd done nothing but drink hot chocolate, eaten fresh bread and cheese, and written for a week, came to mind.

Over the past two years, I'd really upped my knowledge of the business, and my writing acumen. I'd hired outside help in the form of an editor, graphic designer, and publicist. An agent had sought me out and was now helping to publish my books internationally. I had a financial advisor, the same trusted one that Cain used, helping to manage my money and diversify the revenue I brought in. Even though it was against the normal, and I had been scared shitless for much of that first year as a published author, not going to college had been the right decision for me.

I wasn't bogged down by a class schedule, and that was great, because believe me, being an author was a full-time, with overtime available, job. It took a village to write a book, and I was lucky enough to make it my only source of income. I knew how lucky I was to do that, to be able to travel and gain inspiration.

It took all day, every day to grow a business. I wasn't making the big bucks just yet, but I was comfortable, and certainly made more money than I'd ever known growing up. I was squirreling it away, even traveling on a budget when I probably could afford to splurge a little more. But I wanted to support myself, and maybe someday a family, and that kind of salary didn't come overnight.

Sometimes, Mom came on the trips with me. It was a blessing to be able to take her on my adventures, to give back to her for raising me as a single parent. I'd dropped in on her and Michael's honeymoon last year in Hawaii for two days. And I had even gotten Grandma to go to Ireland with me. She was in whiskey heaven, even though she said she couldn't wait to get back home to her ranch.

I make it to my seat with seconds to spare, my lungs almost collapsing in on themselves and my hair a disheveled mess, but I'd made it nonetheless.

"Way to cut it close."

Annabelle turns to me in her seat, a smug smile on her face.

I lean over and hug her, pinching her cheek as revenge for the smart remark. "Good to see you, too, sis."

Anna had decided to attend the same college as Cain, so I got to see her a lot. We'd actually become very close since becoming stepsisters, and when I wasn't trying to get Cain to decorate the apartment with me, Anna helped. She called it training as she was trying to graduate with a degree in interior design.

Yes, our apartment. Cain had begged and begged, and I'd finally given in to moving in together about eight months ago. I had to admit, it was easier than driving back and forth from Haven to Austin three times a week, and I was basically living with the man anyway.

Living together was ... better than I'd expected it to be. Cain had not only come a long way as an athlete, he'd made leaps and bounds as a boyfriend. He cooked us healthy meals, pretended not to be interested when I watched television shows on Bravo, and once a week we picked an audiobook to listen to together. We'd sit on our couch with a glass of wine and listen to the narrators tell us a story. Some books were old, and some were new. But at least once a month we listened to portions of *Great Expectations*. Just for nostalgia's sake.

We made love like our alone time was going out of style, and Cain had started talking to me about marriage and babies. Who the hell would have thought, the bad boy jock I saw climbing out of a soft-top Jeep all of those years ago would be talking about white picket-fencing me?

I wasn't ready for all of that ... but someday I would be. And I'd only be ready for it with Cain.

"Here we go." I breathe as the players run out of the tunnel.

Our seats are in the family section, the same place they always are. I never miss a game, unless a stupid flight gets delayed. Cain's college jersey was sported on my back. It was authentic, except for the tiny piece of fabric on the inside of the left sleeve. A part of his high school jersey, the one I'd worn when the team had won state. I'd had it sewn in as my own little good luck charm.

And there he is, running alongside his teammates, his face

forward and focused. I know, from knowing him inside and out, that he is blocking it all out.

Until, for one split second, he looks up into the stands and catches my eyes.

Those vibrant green charmers hold mine, he grins, and then as quickly as it happened, he is all business once again.

That look is reserved only for me. The only thing that could break him out of his focus.

The only one.

Do you want to know what really happened the night Annabelle slept with Cain?

Read You're the One I Don't Want, the standalone follow up novel featuring Annabelle and Boone!

Do you want your **FREE** Carrie Aarons eBook?

All you have to do is **sign up for my newsletter**, and you'll immediately receive your free book!

ALSO BY CARRIE AARONS

Standalones:

Love at First Fight

Nerdy Little Secret

That's the Way I Loved You

Fool Me Twice

Hometown Heartless

The Tenth Girl

You're the One I Don't Want

Privileged

Elite

Red Card

Down We'll Come, Baby

As Long As You Hate Me

All the Frogs in Manhattan

Save the Date

Melt

When Stars Burn Out

Ghost in His Eyes

On Thin Ice

Kissed by Reality

The Callahan Family Series:

Warning Track

The Rogue Academy Series:

The Second Coming

The Lion Heart

The Mighty Anchor

The Nash Brothers Series:

Fleeting

Forgiven

Flutter

Falter

The Flipped Series:

Blind Landing

Grasping Air

The Captive Heart Duet:

Lost

Found

The Over the Fence Series:

Pitching to Win

Hitting to Win

Catching to Win

Box Sets:

The Complete Captive Heart Duet

The Over the Fence Box Set

ABOUT THE AUTHOR

Author of romance novels such as The Tenth Girl and Privileged, Carrie Aarons writes books that are just as swoon-worthy as they are sarcastic. A former journalist, she prefers the love stories of her imagination, and the athleisure dress code, much better.

When she isn't writing, Carrie is busy binging reality TV, having a love/hate relationship with cardio, and trying not to burn dinner. She's a Jersey girl living in Texas with her husband, daughter, son and Great Dane/Lab rescue.

Please join her readers group, Carrie's Charmers, to get the latest on new books, as well as talk about reality TV, wine and home decor.

You can also find Carrie at these places:

Website

Facebook

Instagram

Twitter

Amazon

Goodreads